Tales from Cameroon

Tales from Cameroon

RENÉ PHILOMBE

Letters from My Hut
and
Cats' Tails Tales
and
"The True Martyr is Me"

*Translated from the French
by Richard Bjornson*

Three Continents Press
Washington, D.C.

© Richard Bjornson 1984

First English Language Edition
   Three Continents Press
   1346 Connecticut Avenue N.W.   3CP
   Washington, D.C. 20036

Original French Language Editions
© René Philombe
   Lettres de ma cambuse, Yaoundé, 1965
   Histoires queue-de-chat, Yaoundé, 1971

ISBN: 0-89410-314-8 (cased)
ISBN: 0-89410-315-6 (paper)
LC No: 84-50629

Illustrations © MAX·KARL Winkler 1984

CONTENTS

Tales from Cameroon

INTRODUCTION

By focusing on common people entangled in webs of social and psychological forces that distort their lives, René Philombe has created a body of literature which raises issues of universal human concern, while remaining firmly rooted in the specific customs of his native Cameroon. The success of his short stories and anecdotes is largely attributable to the artistic sensibility of the perspective from which he views these people. Although he is constantly drawing attention to the folly and injustice which inhibit the emergence of a better, more humane society, he always communicates a sense of compassion for his characters. Even in the smallest details of day-to-day existence, he discovers poignant expressions of the ignorance and hypocrisy which lie behind man's alienation from man. The tragedy of this situation weighs heavily on him, but he never abandons his belief in the possibility of breaking down the barriers which separate people from each other. In fact, he regards his own literary efforts as contributions toward the elimination of barriers. For this reason, his works speak not only to his fellow countrymen, whom he has always considered to be his primary audience, but also to anyone who acknowledges the existence of evil, yet yearns for an equitable society based on truth and a sense of human decency.

The primary values in all Philombe's writings are the same "geniality" and intellectual penetration espoused by Herman Melville, whose attitudes toward the problems of nineteenth-century America are not altogether different from those of Philombe toward modern African society. Like Melville, Philombe advanced these values as fundamental tenets of a passionate wisdom acquired through an awareness of suffering and of death. Behind the artistic sensibility which endows his writing with depth and expressive force, there is the life of a remarkable individual who has survived imprisonment, betrayal, a crippling illness, and the prohibition of his works without becoming embittered or relinquishing his faith in the humanizing power of literature. Throughout his career, Philombe has never lost a wry but compassionate sense of humor, and the dominant tone in all his writings has remained what the eighteenth-century Russian dramatist Gribodoyev once called "laughter through tears." This fusion of the comic and tragic dimensions of life is expressed in a style which combines the clarity and concision of classical French prose with storytelling techniques drawn from

1

African oral traditions. In fact, Philombe's unique sensibility is characterized by the felicitous synthesis of disparate elements, and any reading of his work would be enhanced by an understanding of how this synthesis has emerged, evolved, and found expression in literature.

The selections included in this volume are from three different periods in Philombe's development as a writer. _Letters From My Hut_ was written in the late 1950's when he was struggling to overcome the effects of a serious illness. He had not yet achieved recognition as a writer; his style betrayed the imprint of voluminous readings in classical French literature, and his sense of plot was not yet fully developed, but the keenness of his observations and the profound humanity of his reflections revealed the working of a mind admirably attuned to the nuances and deeper significance of everything it encountered. By the late 1960's, when _Cats' Tails Tales_ appeared, Philombe had become an active force in Cameroonian cultural life. His writings had earned him a rather sizeable audience in his own country, and he had perfected a deceptively simple but subtle and flexible style. Without suppressing the sensitivity which made his first book so charming and so profoundly human, he had also developed a highly controlled sense of plot. The final story, "The True Martyr is Me," was composed to be broadcast on the French National Radio, and it reflects Philombe's growing concern with the structures of social injustice and with their effects on human consciousness. In his earlier tales and anecdotes, he had depicted ignorance and injustice, implying that individuals could change, if they would only recognize the need to see clearly and to act with compassion and kindness. "The True Martyr is Me," however, stresses the process by means of which dehumanizing social structures impose themselves on people's minds. This shift in emphasis reflects Philombe's increasingly urgent desire to speak out against all forms of oppression. He is no longer content to make readers aware of ignorance and injustice; he wants to make them feel the necessity for collective action against the structures which are destroying them spiritually and physically.

I

In _Letters From My Hut_, each story or anecdote consists of three basic components: a provoking scene or incident, the filtering consciousness of an observer attempting to make sense of it, and the implicit moral which the encounter between event and consciousness encourages the reader to draw. Sometimes linked with an aphoristic statement, the initial scene usually involves an example of ignorance compounded by pretentiousness. The situation is then placed in a context of meaning which may include subsequent events, flashbacks, or allegorical parables. Because the original scene is invariably an everyday occurence, it could easily be interpreted as something normal and natural, but because the narrator's inquiring temperament compels him to scrutinize it more intently, he succeeds in stripping away the veil of conventionality which obscures its true significance. In the process, he prods readers to ask: Why must it be this way? Can it be otherwise? His hope is of course that readers will ask the same questions about the world in which they are living.

In anecdotes like "Little Causes, Great Effects," a characteristic type of ignorance emerges in the argument between an adolescent boy and two girls. Their argument over the spelling of a word degenerates first into an exchange of insults and then into an actual fight. However, their altercation is like a pebble cast into a pond. Bystanders find cause for amusement in the affair, and they continue to laugh, even when a respectable older woman loses her dress while attempting to separate the young combatants. Arriving at this moment, her husband sees only the humiliation being heaped on her, and his fury is indiscriminately discharged against the entire crowd. In the ensuing melee, a man is killed. The original dispute was petty; how could it have produced such tragic results? Just as the water in a pond allows ripples to spread, the spectators' indifference to the discomfiture of others permits them to laugh and provides a target for the husband's anger. If they had acted more judiciously to help separate the young people, or if they had acted more compassionately to shield the woman from disgrace, the "little cause" would never have produced such "great effects." The narrator obviously understands this relationship between the attitude of the crowd and the death of a human being, but he doesn't explicitly offer it as an explanation for what happened. Yet his concern contrasts sharply with the spectators' willingness to reduce the young people and the woman to objects of laughter, and by framing the entire episode with a question, he is encouraging readers to formulate a judgment of the situation in their own terms.

Particularly sensitive to injustice and the suffering of others, this narrator always records such events in a way that invites readers to look beyond surface appearances and to feel sympathy for their fellow human beings. Mandari is a middle-aged former prostitute whose nostalgic desire for wealth and adulation contrast with the narrator's detachment from worldly concerns and his yearning for peace; the fact that he is reading Voltaire's *Candide* and feels in harmony with its stoic resignation suggests his state of mind. Nevertheless, as the initial scene of Mandari's eviction is placed into a human context by means of the autobiographical sketch she provides for him, he begins to empathize with her despair and loneliness. Self-righteous observers might condemn her disreputable career and her gaudy make-up, but she is suffering, and the narrator's willingess to address her as "Mademoiselle" becomes an act of kindness, because it suggests that someone still sees her as young and attractive.

In "When the Pupils' Parents Intervene" the narrator's empathy with a young schoolteacher finds expression in the form of indignation at the religious authorities who had removed him from his position for having lived with an unmarried woman. Not only had the young man been an effective teacher under the most difficult circumstances; he had actually been forced to share the woman's apartment to avoid starving on the meager salary they paid him. The narrator is appalled that the young man's talent and good will are being wasted at a time when the country is in desperate need of people like him, but the lack of understanding and compassion on the part of Catholic school officials, who piously preach Christian charity, so blatantly contradicts their own teachings, that in contemplating the parents' reaction to the firing, the narrator feels obliged to reflect upon the principles which should govern the education of children.

3

"Only a climate of love and discipline," he says, "can make the school into a true family within human society." The parents intuitively understand the desirability of creating this sense of community, but the authorities' ignorance and pretentiousness stand in its way. The narrator's emotional response to this state of affairs is built into his account in such a way that readers feel the weight of an idea which he never explicitly states.

The same technique characterizes the two parables in the collection: "Papa Mboya's Bloodthirsty Goat" and "The Dog and the Chimpanzee". In both cases, the theme is the same: animals pretend to be something they are not and betray their fellow creatures for what they believe to be their own self-interest, but in betraying their brothers, they have actually betrayed themselves. For example, Papa Mboya's little goat Moambu associates himself with a pack of hyenas and agrees to lure the farmer's unsuspecting sheep into ambushes. As long as the ruse works, Moambu is treated well and even accorded a certain privilege in hyena society, but when Papa Mboya discerns the truth and takes steps to protect his flock, the hunting expeditions become less fruitful, and the hyenas decide to eat the little goat whom they had formerly honored. The idea for this tale had originally occurred to Philombe during the colonial period, when he witnessed the way in which certain Cameroonian members of the French parliament assured themselves of wealth and social status by traducing the interests of their fellow Africans. Thus, "Papa Mboya's Bloodthirsty Goat" can be interpreted as an allegorical condemnation of self-serving politicians who, having assimilated the cultural values of their colonialist masters, had abandoned the only genuine identity they would ever have.

Yet the significance of "Papa Mboya's Bloodthirsty Goat" runs far deeper than its reference to any specific historical circumstances, because, like "The Dog and the Chimpanzee," it prompts readers to reflect upon the consequences of repudiating that which the narrator obviously values — solidarity with one's fellow creatures and intellectual honesty. In each parable, overblown ambition breeds a pretentiousness which leads to betrayal, but because proud and selfish individuals inevitably fall victim to their own blindness, the reader is being invited to imagine what alternative values the characters might have adopted. Once this possibility has been established, its applicability to the smallest incidents of daily life becomes evident. Are people acting with integrity and a sense of community, and when they are not, wouldn't it be better if they did? These are the sorts of questions which the narrative sensibility in *Tales From My Hut* seeks to stimulate in the minds of sympathetic readers.

II

This sensibility is Philombe himself — a man who passionately identifies with the suffering, disinherited, simple people of Africa and just as passionately cries out against oppression, injustice and cruelty. Always implicitly urging his readers to penetrate false masks and to preserve a feeling for what it is to be human, he fervently believes that literature has an important role to play in the contemporary world. The story of this unique sensibility with its faith in the power of words is nearly as fascinating as the tales which have merged from it. By the time he wrote *Letters From My Hut* in the late 1950's

Philombe was a virtual invalid. He had received no university education, and he had never left Cameroon. Yet he was already an accomplished prose stylist and a homespun moral philosopher imbued with humanistic ideals.

Born in 1930, he was given the name Philippe-Louis Ombedé. His father was a secretary-intepreter in the French colonial administration. An educated, industrious man who could speak several European and African languages, he exerted a strong influence on his young son. After attending a series of lay and Catholic mission schools, Philombe was admitted to the high school in Yaounde, where he excelled in composition, helped edit the school newspaper, and began to write poems and romantic autobiographical fragments based upon French classical models. At this time, he came under the influence of a young history teacher, Madame Jacquot, who introduced him to revolutionary ideas about socialism and social justice. He transformed these ideas into practice and led several hunger strikes; as a consequence , he was expelled from school — his formal education terminated at the age of sixteen!

But Philombe did not stop learning. In fact, his success as a writer stems in part from the fact that he has always taught himself what he wanted to know. After returning to the family farm at Ndji (about sixty miles north of Yaounde), Philombe worked in his father's coffee and tobacco fields, but he also read voluminously, collected oral tales and proverbs, and continued to write. Rather than classroom exercises to be completed as quickly as possible and then forgotten, his intellectual pursuits were joyous excursions into the realm of ideas — ideas which could be related to the world around him and integrated into a deeply felt, personal philosophy of life.

When his father was named president of the traditional court at Saa, his son accompanied him as a personal secretary. Within a year, the quality of his reports had come to the attention of the French commandant, who soon appointed him secretary to the entire tribunal. During this time, Philombe continued to read authors like Voltaire, Montesquieu, La Fontaine, and Baudelaire. He also studied indigenous customs and superstitions, and with the support of the new commandant, he founded a cultural association to preserve folk literature and to provide a forum for the discussion of local traditions. In 1948, he won his first literary prize for a short story based on a Beti folktale. For four years following his expulsion from high school, Philombe had educated himself, and this formative period was crucial to his future development as a writer, for it enabled him to fuse elements of European and Cameroon culture into the personal idiom and philosophy which would later characterize the artistic sensibility in his mature writings.

During the early 1950's, this sensibility was plunged into the realities of anticolonialist political activity. Although he would have preferred to teach modern agricultural methods to farmers, Philombe accepted an administrative appointment in the police. He was posted to the large port city, Douala, where he encountered the leading figures in Cameroon's nascent independence movement. Soon he became involved in union organizing. When he refused to apply for French citizenship, he lost a chance for advancement in the colonial administration, and when he attended a political rally in British Cameroon, he was threatened with disciplinary sanctions, which were only averted by the last-minute intervention of a French superior, who effected his

5

transfer to Yaounde.

Philombe's work gave him ample opportunity to observe the inequities of colonialist oppression but it also placed him in contact with the life conditions and superstitions of the variegated masses who passed through the police station each day, and it inspired him with a firm belief in the necessity of providing institutional guarantees so that all people would be treated equally before the law. At about this time, he petitioned the United Nations in the name of the people from his region of Cameroon, demanding reparations from the French government for their exploitation of an enormous tobacco plantation situated on arbitrarily appropriated tribal lands. As the result of an unprecedented legal decision, his people won the case, and the French were ordered to pay more than $30,000 to the community of Batchenga, but once again Philombe had incurred the displeasure of the colonial authorities. However, in a very real sense, he had merely absorbed the egalitarian ideals of the French political tradition and demanded that they be applied to Africans as well as to Frenchmen.

Guided by such convictions, Philombe would undoubtedly have participated in the increasingly violent liberation struggle which broke out in many parts of Cameroon during the late 1950's, but in 1955 he experienced the first symptoms of what was later diagnosed as a spinal tumor. Pain wracked his body, and for long periods of time, he remained confined to a hospital bed. During his three year convalescence, he rented a small house in the Nlong-Kak section of Yaounde. To fill countless hours of forced leisure, he wrote lengthy epistles to his friend and doctor, Zogo-Massey. In them, he described the apparently trivial events which comprised the life of the neighborhood, and he adapted folk tales and anecdotes that he recalled from his earlier days at Ndji and at Saa. These letters were enlivened by Philombe's sharp eye for significant detail, his wry sense of humor, and his strong commitment to human decency and justice. Without sacrificing the uniquely individual qualities of the persons he depicted, he managed to show how their desires and fears had a universal human significance. Written between 1956 and 1958, these letters were never intended for publication, but their wit, perceptiveness, and purity of style were so impressive that when Editions CLE (francophone Africa's first important publishing house) was founded in Yaounde, its editors chose to inaugurate their literature series by issuing them as *Lettres de ma cambuse (Letters From My Hut)*. Their choice was a good one, for the book was later awarded the prestigious Prix Mottart of the French Academy.

Although Philombe's characteristic style and sensibility are already apparent in *Letters From My Hut*, these early letters represent merely the first stage in his growth as a writer. Unable to participate physically in the events that culminated in Cameroon's independence, he nevertheless remained fully committed to his countryman's struggle for freedom and dignity. After a brief period of depression, he founded and edited two newspapers devoted to raising the consciousness of the Cameroonian masses: *La Voix du citoyen* in French and *Bebelu Ebug* in Ewondo. In the columns of these publications, he defended his egalitarian, humanistic viewpoints and began to employ a mildly satiric style to excoriate abuses of wealth and power, to deflate pretentiousness, to unmask hypocrisy, and to attack the retrogressive tendencies of traditional superstitions. It was at this time that he adopted the pen name René Philombe. Derived from the verb "renaître" (to be born again), the name "René" reflects his conviction that every individual is "born again" when he decides to lead a public life; it also suggests his own "rebirth" after a long period of physical suffering and mental depression. "Philombe" is simply a contraction of his given name Philippe-Louis Ombedé. When asked why he had not chosen a more typically Cameroonian name, he replied that, like it or not, all Africans who had attended European schools and written in European languages owed nearly as much to Europe as they did to Africa. His response was not intended as a repudiation of his African heritage, but as an assertion of his identity as a person whose consciousness had been shaped by several cultures.

Philombe's two newspapers reached a circulation of over 5,000 and soon allowed him to become self-supporting, but the fervently independent and critical attitudes of his articles frequently offended the authorities. On at least six occasions before and after Independence, he was arbitrarily arrested and imprisoned. Such treatment severely aggravated the physical infirmities which already made it virtually impossible for him to walk. Despite these harrassments, Philombe maintained his avid interest in cultural affairs. During the late 1950's, two young schoolteachers often visited him in Nlong-Kak, and the three of them spent long hours discussing French literature and traditional Cameroonian customs; they also read their own poems, riddles and short stories to each other. One of the teachers baptized their meeting place "Odéon," and that was the name under which Philombe's "hut" subsequently became known.

When the government sponsored an exhibition of Cameroon art as part of the independence celebrations in 1960, the three young men seized the opportunity to become acquainted with other aspiring writers. A short time later, Philombe called them all together at the "Odéon," and the Association of Cameroonian Writers and Poets was formed. He himself was elected secretary-general of the new organization — a post he held for over twenty years — and from that moment until the present, he has worked tirelessly to promote Cameroonian letters by keeping alive the association's occasional journal, *Cameroun littéraire*, by editing its excellent anthology of Cameroonian poetry, and by encouraging the numerous younger writers who came to him for aid and advice. As a result of his refusal to bow to political pressure and his insistence on saying openly what he believes privately, Philombe has become an almost legendary figure for a great many of the country's more idealistic students.

In his own country, therefore, Philombe is a moral force and an animator of cultural activity, but he has always considered himself primarily as a writer. Even in prison he composed a collection of poems. And on the several occasions when he returned to Ndji, where he helped organize several peasant cooperatives, he found the leisure to complete two novels— *Sola ma chérie* (1966) and *Un sorcier blanc à Zangali* (1969) — and the short stories which would later be published as *Histoires queue-de-chat* (1970). These are the stories presented in this volume as *Cats' Tails Tales*, and

7

they demonstrate the enormous progress that Philombe had made in characterization and narrative technique since writing the tales and anecdotes included in his letters to Dr. Zogo-Massey. His deceptively simple style remains the same, and the background sensibility which continually invites readers to contemplate the reasons behind everyday examples of folly and injustice is still present, but the sorts of observations and anecdotes that were reported with minimal elaboration in *Letters From My Hut* are no more than raw materials for the richly textured storeis in *Cats' Tails Tales*. Drawing on scenes he had witnessed in Yaounde and in Ndji, Philombe transformed fragmentary impressions and incidents into well-formed stories which abundantly fulfilled the Horatian admonition to entertain and instruct.

III

Each of the five stories in *Cats' Tails Tales* focuses on one of the many superstitions which blind people to their true nature and which, like "iron balls on the legs of slaves," impede their progress toward a better and more humane world. As in *Letters From My Hut*, the author eschews abstract moralizing, although the words and actions of the characters are always filtered through the story-teller's consciousness in such a way that readers are encouraged to reflect on the causes of folly. In the tales of "Cats' Tails," however, this effect is amplied by the recurrence of a narrative structure which draws attention to the quite unmysterious chain of events leading from superstitious belief to gullibility to unpleasant or tragic consequences.

In every case, the story opens with a general observation or question that is linked with a specific scene, the full significance of which usually does not emerge until the end of the narrative. For example, in "The Sango Mbedi Affair," the narrator begins by declaring that "a police summons is never read in quite the same way as a love letter." This unexceptional pronouncement is used to introduce a description of Madame Tina's departure from her comfortably furnished house in a respectable neighborhood of Yaounde. A fashionable and successful prostitute, Madame Tina feels confident that her summons involves some routine matter like an unpaid traffic ticket. As Police Chief Engamba's interrogation proceeds, however, his reconstruction of her involvement with the convicted embezzler Sango Mbedi threatens to destroy her composure, for she had personally compiled a list of important government functionaries to aid a sorcerer in fulfilling his promise to eradicate all documents relating to the case against Mbedi. When she could not raise the money to pay the sorcerer, he had taken the list to the prime minister and accused her of having hired him to assassinate the people named on it. Ultimately the machinations of the sorcerer were unmasked, and a badly shaken Madame Tina escaped with a reprimand and a word of warning against the fraudulent promises of sorcerers. As readers reflect back on this chain of events, the narrator's opening comment takes on a new meaning. Not only does Madame Tina's experience at the police station demonstrate why a summons can never be read in the same manner as a love letter, it underlines two different perspectives on her dealings with the dishonest sorcerer. On the earnest entreaty of her former lover Sango Mbedi, she had originally sought out the "professor," but rather than a "love letter" of appreciation, all she received in return was an impersonal summons. Yet, as someone who sold her affections for money and rejected the possibility of love and trust, she only got what she deserved, especially in light of the fact that Mbedi, whom she affected to disdain after his fall from power, was probably in league with the sorcerer from the very beginning. Madame Tina's initial obliviousness to the distinction between a love letter and a summons thus takes on a doubly ironic significance.

Similar linkages between general observations and specific scenes occur near the beginning of every story in *Cats' Tails Tales*. Interest is generated by piqueing the readers' curiosity to know more about the scene, what lay behind it, and how it related to the narrator's general commentary. The answers to such questions inevitably lie in a preceding episode which involved some form of witchcraft; therefore, each story relies on one or more flashbacks to place the opening scene in perspective. Because Philombe regards witchcraft as a fraudulent trick perpetrated on gullible individuals, the structure of these flashbacks is always quite similar: first, a context of superstitious beliefs is established, and then a motivation for resorting to them is gradually revealed. For example in "Bekamba, Returned from the Dead," the villagers of Mangata are willing to believe that a man could die and return to life. Fearing that he might be held responsible for his cousin's death after their dug-out canoe had capsized and left him marooned for six months on an island in the middle of the Sanaga River, Bekamba fabricates a story to fit their system of superstitious beliefs. He had, he claimed, visited the land of the phantoms and learned the wishes and secrets of the ancestors. At first, he demands little or nothing for imparting his knowledge and power to others, but when his hut begins to attract pilgrims from a wide area, Bekamba becomes wealthy and Mangata prospers. In the process, the charlatan's motivation changed from fear to the desire for money and prestige.

For most of the self-styled prophets, sorcerers and witchdoctors in *Cats' Tails Tales*, the latter motivation was present from the beginning, and when Philombe focuses on a victim of their confidence tricks, the willingness to be duped often proves to be an outgrowth of the same acquisitiveness and social ambition. In "Dr. Tchumba's Little Snake," for example, the gullible peasant Ndoumna Cyriac entrusts his mother's life savings to a wandering sorcerer in the hope that he will become rich, and he wants to become rich, because he is jealous of a former classmate, a civil servant who occasionally returns to Mfou and parades his wealth before the admiring eyes of the villagers. Like all the other stories in this collection, "Dr. Tchumba's Little Snake" evokes the system of folk belief according to which a particular superstition supposedly makes sense. In this context, dishonest individuals can easily manipulate appearances to abuse the credulity of simple people, although the victims of their ruses are, like Ndoumna, generally motivated by their own selfish desires. The second phase of Philombe's narrative structure thus draws attention to the two human weaknesses which contribute most to the perpetuation of charlatanry: ignorance and selfishness.

During the final phase, the narrator pursues the action introduced in the opening scene and, against a background provided by the flashback, reveals the actual results of an overly credulous belief in the supernatural powers of sorcerers. By juxtaposing the narrator's account of events with the sorcerer's preposterous claims, the folly of such belief becomes apparent, but Philombe is interested in a far more important goal than simply debunking popular superstitions. He wants to show that both deceiver and deceived are victimized in a deeper psychological sense by the climate of ignorance and selfishness that encourages some people to prey on others. The sorcerer's dupes always suffer loss and anxiety. Ndoumna Cyriac forfeits an enormous sum of money, and the serpent he imagines to be gnawing at his stomach becomes an appropriate symbol for the jealousy which originally impelled him to seek the aid of a sorcerer. Madame Tina's involvement with witchcraft leads only to difficulties with the police and the fear that she will be punished for a crime she never committed.

However, the charlatans too are victims of their own states of mind. Both Bekamba and the sorcerer in "Dr. Tchumba's Little Snake" contend that "life belongs to those who know how to take care of themselves." They interpret this typically Western aphorism in a quite materialistic sense, but if a cynical self-reliance can be used to justify their ingenious ruses, it also effectively cuts them off from any *genuine* sense of community and makes them vulnerable to institutional pressures from the society in which they are no more than parasites. Despite momentary successes, the sorcerer himself proves to be a ludicrously lonely and alienated individual—a fact which becomes abundantly clear when characters like Bekamba and Madame Tina's "professor" are confronted by an official scrutiny of their affairs. Because their supposed power to control events is a sham, they lose their composure and reveal themselves to be small-minded, cowardly people. In this way, the recurrent narrative structure in *Cats' Tails Tales* reinforces the narrator's implicit condemnations of deceivers and deceived, but the final conclusion is always reserved for the readers, who must articulate for themselves the moral and intellectual values according to which the characters and their beliefs deserve the judgments that have obviously been passed on them.

For Philombe, these values remain the same as those which characterized the narrative sensibility in *Letters From My Hut* — intellectual honesty, compassion, and a sense of community. Although never explicitly defined as virtues, such qualities are

subtly woven into each story. Throughout *Cats' Tails Tales* the tacit assumption is that, if the characters could only share the objective viewpoint of the narrator and the implied reader, they would recognize that people don't return from the dead, that men can die from natural causes, that lightning and eclipses are perfectly natural phenomena. that anyone who could conjure up unlimited amounts of money would never need to be paid for his services. In other words, readers are being conditioned to demand an intellectually rigorous appraisal of surface appearances.

Similarly, there are examples of compassion and communal spirit. In "Old Mbarta's Two Daughters," a formerly pretentious and lonely man is rescued from his decaying hut by the solicitude of his fellow villagers, who carry him to the hospital and build him a new house. He himself is reconciled with his daughters, not so much because a curse has been placed on them, but because he feels their suffering and rises to their defense when the villagers inflict punishments on them. Old Mbarta is a man who acquires wisdom through suffering, but perhaps the greatest hero in *Cats' Tails Tales* is Dr. Tchumba. Roughly based on Philombe's brother, to whom the book is dedicated, Tchumba resembles the various portrayals of Ed Ricketts in the novels and autobiographical essays of John Steinbeck. With a shrewd intellectual penetration, Tchumba diagnoses the psychosomatic origins of Ndoumna's malady and devises an appropriate cure. He recognizes the young peasant's ignorance and gullibility, but he refrains from mocking him; in fact, he treats him with compassion and understanding. Such actions and the attitudes behind them provide clues to the positive, humanistic values which permeate Philombe's entire work, but they remain clues which need to be identified, interpreted, and applied by others. As a consumate story-teller who is also a moralist, Philombe engages readers in the process of judgment; he does not make judgments for them.

IV

One of the principal themes in Philombe's work during the 1950's and 1960's was blindness — people's blindness to themselves and to their potential for leading decent lives based on intellectual honesty and a sense of community. This blindness was nourished by a climate of ignorance, fear, and pretentiousness, but the focus of the implicit narrative commentary was generally fixed on the individual's capacity to see. The implication was that, if people would simply become more aware, they could choose to act differently. There were hints of an underlying social injustice: the young schoolteacher in *Letters From My Hut* did lose his position as the result of an arbitrary administrative decision, Bekamba and Madame Tina were subjected to frightening police interrogations, and the young heroes of Philombe's novel *Sola ma chérie* were victimized in part by the institution of the dowry. Yet the structural inequities and abuses of power behind these events remained in the background. They did occupy a prominent place in his political poetry, but it circulated primarily in mimeographed form and among small groups of friends. For example, the poems he wrote during the early 1960's in a Yaounde prison did not reach a larger audience until they were published as *Choc-Antichoc* in 1978. Because political corruption and social injustice have always been sensitive topics in Cameroon, writers living there have tended to avoid them as subjects for serious literary treatment. With the publication of *Choc-Antichoc*, the play *Africapolis* (about the fall of a degenerate African dictator), and the novel *L'Ancien maquisard* (about the disillusionment and despair of a former guerilla fighter who returns to society after a long political imprisonment), Philombe broke this taboo. Although his brief radio drama, "The True Martyr is Me," is ostensibly about an event from the colonialist past, it too illustrates the new thrust of Philombe's writing by foregrounding the corruption of a socio-political system and the effects of that system on human consciousness.

What prompted Philombe to adopt a more overt form of social criticism? For him personally, this stance is not without danger, but he feels compelled to take it, because he is convinced that literature will lose its power to humanize, if it fails to deal honestly with the crucial issues of its own time. Like Achebe and Ngugi, he no longer regards the traditional anticolonialist struggle as the most fruitful theme for contemporary African literature. To be sure, he recognizes the need to overcome the legacy of colonialism, and he remains willing to draw his subject matter from the colonialist era, but his real concern is with the present social structure and the attitudes engendered by it. This new emphasis in his work derives from his own experiences of injustice; perhaps it also reflects the increased self-assurance of a writer who has achieved international recognition and feels more intensely the obligations of his role as the moral conscience of his people; certainly it relates to a sense of urgency — a belief that he has something important to say and that he can say it best in the literary forms he has perfected during the past twenty years.

Since 1965, Philombe has received a number of literary prizes and awards. His works have been translated into German, English, Italian, Russian, and Romanian. He has been interviewed by journalists and scholars from four continents. But even such international recognition has not sheltered him from reprisals by political authorities who resent his independence of mind. He was once arrested for having been elected traditional head of the people in his area of Cameroon; his house has been searched repeatedly, and he has lost many of his papers and manuscripts. In 1974, he was refused permission to stage *Africapolis* in Yaounde, and in 1978, he was informed that *L'Ancien Maquisard* would not be allowed to circulate in Cameroon. Despite such difficulties, however, he has persevered in his efforts to create an atmosphere of free and honest cultural expression in his native country. On three occasions since 1970, Philombe has helped found theater troupes to produce plays by local authors. He was instrumental in creating the short-lived but highly innovative *Ozila*, a literary review which sought to encourage creativity and to awaken critical consciousness by publishing both imaginative works and evaluative interpretations of them. Between 1972 and 1975, he supported himself by organizing and operating a book shop, "Sémences Africaines", in the Mvog-Mbi section of Yaounde. While working there, he continued to write poems, plays, short stories, and novels, and he began work on *The Cameroon Book and Its Authors*, the first complete and reliable history of Cameroon literature. Writers gathered at "Sémences Africaines" to discuss and to exchange ideas. Once again Philombe was at the center of a literary circle, but politically motivated harrassment by the fiscal authorities obliged him to close the doors of his shop and retire to Ndji. Since 1977, however, he has returned to Yaounde, where he is presently employed by the UNESCO-sponsored Regional Center for the Promotion of African Books.

Against this background, Philombe's writings have grown increasingly militant. His basic values have remained the same, but rather than attacking the fabric of individual beliefs and supersititions which prevent people from progressing toward a better world, he has begun to focus on the institutional corruption which many Africans take for granted. In fact, the true subject of *Africapolis, L'Ancien maquisard,* and *Choc-Antichoc* is controlled outrage at the fact that injustice can be taken for granted, and it is this outrage which characterizes the narrator's sensibility in "The True Martyr is Me."

As in the *Cats' Tails Tales,* this story opens with a concrete scene, the meaning of which is clarified in a series of flashbacks, but the full significance of which only becomes apparent when an action emerging from that scene culminates in tragedy and insight. For three years Edanga had been unable to live with the woman he had married in a traditional ceremony, because she had been confined to the "sixa," a curious institution invented by Catholic missionaries in French West Africa. Before any woman could receive the sacrament of marriage, she had to spend an indeterminate amount of time in a special compound at the mission. The compound was called a "sixa", and the ostensible reason for its existence was moral and spiritual instruction, but because the women worked in the fields of the mission, they were sometimes kept there for unreasonably long periods and exploited for their labor. The "sixa" was deeply resented by many Cameroonians, and Mongo Beti wrote a scathingly satiric attack on the practice in his *Poor Christ of Bomba* (1957).

However, none of this is known to readers of "The True Martyr is Me," when Edanga's mother calls out his name on a peaceful Sunday morning in the village of Nsam. His dispirited behavior and ill-tempered responses seem quite unmotivated in light of her good-natured solicitude, but the reasons for his attitude emerge, as it becomes clear that he is preparing to visit his fiancée, who has been at the "sixa" in the Mbankolo mission for three years. His anger at his mother is merely the displacement of his smouldering resentment at a system which has imposed an intolerable separation on him and his "wife." His irrascibility and his refusal to change his dirty clothes suggest that a change has taken place inside Edanga. He is not acting as he had acted on similar occasions, and when he stands up "like a slave who intends to obey only his own whims," he has already decided to rebel against an oppresive system, although he knows neither how it operates nor why it operates as it does. He only knows that he wants his "wife" and that he intends to defy the system which is keeping her captive. His impulse is just. Yet it is doomed to frustration, for he fails to realize that the injustice inflicted on him will exist as long as the system which sanctions it remains in place. And that system will not be overthrown by the courageous but isolated and ignorant act of an individual who lacks the support of his fellow victims. When Edanga drinks to steel himself for the attempted abduction of his wife, he removes inhibitions inculcated in him by a long conditioning process, but he also clouds his understanding of the larger context which has made his unhappiness possible. He succeeds in breaching the wall that had been erected to separate African men from their fiancées in the visiting room, and he succeeds in dragging his wife from the "sixa," but when he kills a priest who had attacked him, Edanga brings about his own death. The Africans in the courtyard might have helped him escape, but they had been indoctrinated by the system; their only concern was to avoid complications for themselves. Without their support, his rebellion remains no more than an heroically futile gesture.

As the culmination of an action introduced in the opening scene, this gesture also reveals the full significance of Edanga's initially puzzling behavior. Even the tragic outcome of his trip to Mbankolo is foreshadowed in the mother's remark that her son's hut appeared "silent as a grave," when he did not reply to her appeals. Philombe's carefully constructed narrative thus underlines the apparent failure of Edanga's attempt to defy an unjust system; however, this same narrative framework endows Edanga's futile gesture with a genuinely revolutionary meaning. The opening scene focuses on Edanga's awakening. He is angry, and anger is the motivating force behind any rebellion. It enables him to disregard precedents which had previously been considered sacrosanct. No man had ever broken through the artificial barrier which the church placed between African men and their fiancées. No one had ever struck a priest, even when the latter was obviously involved in perpetuating an unjust system. Once broken, such taboos lost much of their original force, for even if the people did not support Edanga, they knew they were subject to the same injustice he had suffered, and they had become aware of a new precedent: the unthinkable had been thought, and Edanga's example would live in their memories.

To preserve the significance of his act, however, he had to reject the priest's dying plea that the authorities exercise leniency in dealing with the man who had killed him. The priest sees himself as a martyr dying for a sacred cause, and that is precisely the version of the truth which Edanga can not accept, because it implies the righteousness of the system against which he himself had rebelled. For this reason, he insists that he, not the priest, is the true martyr. Bound up like a sausage and savagely beaten by the police, he is defending his own integrity when he shouts, "the true martyr is me!" His defiance represents a true change of consciousness; it is an awakening which echoes and gives added meaning to the awakening at the beginning of the story.

As in *Cats' Tails Tales*, the narrative framework and narrator sensibility combine to move readers toward a heightened awareness about the world around them, but in contrast to the earlier stories, "The True Martyr is Me" also moves them toward a recognition that individual awareness is not enough. Unjust social systems are perpetuated by force and by the general acceptance of myths which justify the established order. "The True Martyr is Me" serves as an antidote to such myths, unmasking their fraudulent claims and hidden contradictions. If the people can be brought to understand the underlying weakness of a system based on false and hypocritical premises, their own anger does not have to remain impotent, for enlightened collective action, Philombe implies, can change the system. The thrust of this story and much of Philombe's latest work is thus decidedly revolutionary in its implications.

V

During the past twenty years Philombe's narrative technique has undergone a perceptible evolution, and the focus of his writing has shifted, but his deeply felt humanism, his passionate energy, his concern for the craft of writing, and his belief in the importance of literature have remained constant from his earliest letters and sketches to his latest poems, plays, novels, and short stories. In an age when selfishness, hypocrisy, and injustice seem to prevail, writers (according to Philombe) incur an obligation to keep alive visions of a better, more humane world. By honestly portraying the present state of society, he himself strips away the respectable facades behind which people hide their ignorance and egotism. By prodding his readers into drawing their own conclusions about such portrayals, he encourages others to formulate the values on which he believes "tomorrow's world" can be built: love, truth, freedom, justice, productive work. He knows he is yearning toward an ideal that can never be reached, but he persists in pursuing it, because he is convinced that the pursuit of an ideal enables people to demonstrate their humanity.

His own literary career has revolved around the drama of self-discovery. In the introduction to *Letters From My Hut,* he wrote that his eyes were "fixed on the world of men" while his heart was "straining toward the mysterious dark shades of the invisible." When asked what he meant by the "invisible," he smilingly replied, "the self." He feels that there is something deeply mysterious and extremely precious about the phenomenon of human consciousness, but he also knows that most people avoid contact with the innermost recesses of their own being. In a short poem to be declaimed on the moon, he ironically characterized modern man:

> He wants to penetrate the mysteries
> of what lies beyond
> however
> confronted by his own mystery
> he yawns.

To counteract this insensitivity, he proposes in another poem to write the

> . . . song of man
> To create man
> In the heart of man.

This short verse might almost serve as an epigram for Philombe's entire literary enterprise, because he has repeatedly said that he desires above all to remind people of their own humanity.

Even more than self-discovery, he wants his readers to recognize the equivalent of their own selfhood in others. For him, African problems are human problems, and in any society where people are obsessed by the blind pursuit of money, status, or power, they will be plagued by alienation, loneliness, and anxiety. Thus, it is not a question of choosing between traditional African customs and Western ones. On the contrary, what

16

is needed is a judicious winnowing of that which is best in each culture. Without relinquishing a pride in one's African heritage, one can still condemn superstitions and unproductive modes of behavior. Similarly, Africans can learn from Western society without abandoning themselves to materialism and acquisitive individualism. This balanced outlook is embodied in Philombe's own temperament. Born in suffering and an awareness of death, tempered by compassion, and molded by dedication, his humanistic spirit reverberates through even the shortest anecdotes in *Letters From My Hut* and motivates his involvement in Cameroonian cultural affairs. Philombe's stories will continue to be read, because they are good stories, and his impact upon the literary life of his country is immeasurable. Yet, in many ways, his greatest contribution lies in having expressed a sensibility which offers a way out of the spiritual malaise that afflicts such a large part of the contemporary world. "Men are marching toward a universal brotherhood," he once said, "and universal brotherhood is the basis of all true culture."

LETTERS FROM MY HUT

I

MY RETREAT

Nlong-Kak, which means "ox-grass" in *Beti,** owes its somewhat harsh name to an enormous, formerly uncultivated savanna where Hausa cowherds used to graze their cattle.

Administrative buildings now occupy that place as if to establish a sharply defined boundary between the tumultuous splendors of the urban center and the peace of this somewhat gloomy section of town. Once past the intersection known as the *Carrefour de l'Epicerie,* everything changes almost without transition. Each object and each living creature bears a rustic imprint. During working hours the streets are deserted. There are few people, and they walk slowly, dragging their feet. Vehicular traffic thins out and business comes to a standstill.

Besides the road running off to the Bastos factory, and the highway to the North, which divides the neighborhood into two sections, not a single alley there is acquainted with the comfort and salubrity of asphalt paving.

At night, no lights. During the long dry season, the laterite soil engenders the suffocating spectacle of ubiquitous dust clouds. And when the rains come, people flounder about in a sticky mud. That's why the few whitewashed houses were stained with large red splash-marks. Perhaps that's also why the number of modern structures could be counted on one's fingers. . . ! But the fact is that with their minuscule dimensions, with their unpainted mud walls, with their smoke-blackened, raffia-mat roofs, most of the houses in Nlong-Kak have such a woe-begone air that a newly arrived stranger would think himself in a country village.

And I who love the countryside . . . !

In the evening, the sun plunges like a golden disc into the clouds which form halos over the hills surrounding the Bastos plateau. A reddish-brown gleam spreads softly across the trees, shrouding them in a magnificent muslin. Little by little, all movement ceases, and sleep prevails in the huts.

At daybreak, there are no harsh noises to force you awake. First, the cocks sound their punctual reveille at long intervals; a dog barks in a courtyard, a bell tolls at church,

---

*family of languages spoken by tribes collectively known as the Beti of South Central Cameroon

and a drum booms hollowly somewhere. Then, human voices begin to murmur in the early morning shadows.

The narrow promenade, laid out on a raised embankment, will soon become increasingly animated with women, and with women alone. It's a small market place. Hidden beneath a forest of menacing palm trees, it prides itself on its enormous open shed, made from prefabricated segments and covered with sheets of corrugated metal. However, the activity is limited and rather short-lived, for by ten o'clock, no one but the municipal caretaker is visible — an uncouth, rustic fellow with his tattered rags, his wide hat, and his long-handled broom. Until the fall of evening, and even well into the night, he will be throwing clods of dirt at stray chickens, pigs, sheep and dogs — intrusive tenants of never-occupied market stalls.

With a printing plant and a tobacco factory, Nlong-Kak represents an undeniable industrial power in the city of Yaounde. With its Greek Orthodox, Catholic, Presbyterian and Seventh-Day Adventist missions (which peacefully divide up the four cardinal points of the compass), Nlong-Kak is and continues to be a picturesque palette of denominational tendencies, all of which gives one food for thought . . . .

*

*   *

For a soul surfeited with the exhausting hubbub of the urban center, this remote section of the city is just what is needed to promote a treatment for relaxing the nerves. Here such a soul would find all the necessary conditions for a stay in the country. Here too it would be able to taste many beauties of the peasant life.

Nearly everywhere are smiling vegetable gardens from which a thousand sylvan perfumes emanate and where indefatigable, endlessly-singing gardeners go about their daily tasks . . . . Ah! you should hear these beautiful heroines as they warble their stirring laments . . . ! They sing their joys and their sorrows. They sing their dreams and their loves, but most of all, they sing their love of tilling the earth.

It is not rare, moreover, for a folkloric group to enliven the atmosphere by sending nostalgic chants to float in the air. The trees and bushes are inhabited by cuckoos, partridges, guinea hens, and hedgehogs; neither bush fire, nor hunting party would be lacking in the middle of Nlong-Kak to make this urban agglomeration into a veritable rural area silently grafted to the Cameroonian capital.

I am the obscure tenant of a tumbledown shack. Quite proud of its decrepitude, it squats on the edge of the former "German Highway." It bears no grudges against anyone — neither the public fountain which splashes joyously in front of it, nor the pretty little market place which is often laughing in the bright sunshine.

The room I inhabit is a narrow and gloomy sort of refuge which reminds many people of an old sorcerer's den. It is humbly covered with old raffia mats. Adjacent to a kitchen, it is smothered daily beneath wreaths of smoke, because the dividing wall is riddled with gaping crevices. The minuscule back door opens onto a small, sunken enclosure and offers me a pleasant view of gardens and fields, bordered in the distance by the Mfoundi River.

Each morning, I install myself on the porch. There, sprawled in the nonchalance of a lounge-chair, I forget myself on the wing of time. Upon occasion, I tire of reading some endless passage, and to refresh the spirit, I allow my eyes to frisk about in the distance and scan the neighborhood.

Many and varied are the scenes which keep me awake. In the market place, if a passerby slips on a banana peel and falls, how many savage jeers rise up immediately, accompanied by a hammering of old crates! My God, is it a crime to lose one's balance? On the road, if a bicyclist goes head over heels, how many spectators mechanically cry out: *"Awu nono!"* (Death take him!). Charity, where are you? At one moment, women are fighting at the public fountain; they are quarreling over water which flows from the sky generously enough to quench every thirst! At another, a thunder of shouts announces the lightning-like flight of a thief whose legs are accessories, seeking to transport him quickly beyond the reach of public judgment. Yes, it's natural for men to flee dishonor after having knocked at her door, isn't it?

Most of my visitors are from rustic nations: toads, crickets, dragonflies, centipedes, not to mention spiders, flies, and mosquitoes. I lodge all these uncivilized guests to the best of my ability. The wise man should learn to love inferior creatures, if he fears that worms might be reserving an overly harsh welcome for him in the grave.

Numerous other tenants — mice — proliferate around me. For nothing in the world would I accept the renewal of their lease.

More than any other species of parasite, mice exhibit an insufferable effrontery and impertinence. They keep themselves so busy that I wonder if they don't somehow escape the laws of sleep. Night and day, they are constantly on the move. In groups of three or four, they dart in a frenzied manner from their holes. First, they regard me mischievously; then, they conspire among themselves before sniffing about the cupboard, attracted by its tempting odors.

Nothing about my attitude escapes them. My look, my position, my smallest gestures alert them with a surprising accuracy to my intentions. My gallant mice know that, if I am nonchalantly spread out on my bed or cramped behind my little desk, I am incapable of making war on them. But if I dare get up or take hold of my cane, frrrt. . . ! There they go, taking themselves off in a single bound. No human performance could equal the rapidity of their flight. Nevertheless, how could I prevent myself from jeering at such faint-hearted cowardice?

People frequently think that longevity belongs to excessively prudent souls. The truth of that is repeatedly verified under my very eyes. As a matter of fact, with the exception of three naive fellows, my mouse-trap hardly distinguished itself by making any significant catches. While the mice create a hellish rumbling by trotting under my bed, behind my chests, and between the mats, by constantly burrowing through the walls like militiamen on maneuvers and swarming over every nook and cranny in the place — while they're doing all this, I am convinced that the whole fabled *tribe of mice* has taken up residence in my hut.

But, how comfortable I am in this out-of-the-way hut! Instead of good soup, I nourish myself on peace and meditation. Instead of warm clothes, I cover myself with shadow and silence. It's in this mysterious comfort, Reader, that I amuse myself by tracing out these lines, my eyes fixed upon the world of men, but my heart straining toward the mysterious dark shades of the invisible.

II

LITTLE CAUSES, GREAT EFFECTS

The siren had just sounded at the "Bastos" factory. Traffic became animated. The atmosphere grew heavy under the blazing sun which beat down on a babbling, swarming crowd of school children returning home. There was nothing to indicate that the population would forego the pleasure of a peaceful siesta that day.

Deserted since nine o'clock in the morning, the small market place was about to experience a most eventful half-hour. No one suspected it.

The principal actors? Three school children — one boy and two girls. Classmates, they began by discussing the spelling of a word. . .

"Me," said Abondo, "I wrote 'p-o-mm-e'."*

"Aha!" exclaimed Miss Biloa, "you wrote that word wrong . . . !"

"Sure enough," seconded Miss Atouba, "he wrote it wrong, because it's supposed to be the fruit, not 'hand'. In that case, one should write 'p-a-u-m-e'."*

"How can that be?" asked Abondo, astonished and with a pensive air. The teacher taught us that word less than a week ago, and I still remember the exact spelling. It's 'p-o-mm-e' all right!"

The two girls burst out laughing again and uttered a series of mocking "ahas!" But the boy, who had no intention of admitting to an error, teased his companions mercilessly.

"Yes," he said, "it's easy to see that once classes are finished, you girls throw your books and notebooks into the corner and merely gad about the streets of Yaounde!"

"You should talk!" returned Miss Atouba, "And what do you have to say about that letter you dared send to my little sister Ngali? A love letter . . . !"

This altercation, fueled by reciprocal insults and curses, soon degenerated into an unequal combat.

And while blows are being exchanged, a great number of bystanders come running. But they don't come to curb the two girls, who are relentlessly attacking the boy. Cynically, they see it as a pleasant occasion to laugh heartily and amuse

---

*The young pupils were confusing the French near homonyms "pomme" (apple) and "paume" (palm of the hand).

themselves, as if they were at some entertaining theatrical production. Everyone encourages the young combatants with well-chosen curses, which only add fuel to the fire.

There is only one woman, who, respectable by virtue of her age and corpulence, threads her way among the little demons. Herself the mother of children, she places herself between the warring parties in an attempt to reconcile them. But she goes about it the wrong way.

Indeed, the boy alone withdraws at the first summons. In contrast, the two girls are like inconsolable Amazons. Hearts boiling with anger, they still want to pursue the battle. Furiously they attach themselves to the good woman's dress, which is soon reduced to rags.

The crowd's laughter redoubles. No one tries to ward off the scandal. People wriggle about, jostle each other, and joyously clap their hands all around this mother of a family, this innocent victim of public rudeness.

Meanwhile, a forty-year-old man, out of breath and speechless with rage, bursts onto the scene.

"My wife stark naked in public?" he sputters.

The furious man elbows his way through the crowd. Then, with all the ferocity that indignation and anger supply to the human spirit, he brings his head and shoulders into action, his arms and legs, even his buttocks. . . . A direct jab to this person, an uppercut to that one, a kick to another one . . . . He distributes blows at random and attacks the entire brood of ill-mannered onlookers.

Others come spontaneously to the assistance of the offended woman. At that moment, a savage brawl breaks out . . . .

A brawl of unbridled horses hurling themselves blindly at each other. A brawl of wild beasts attacking frontally and biting each other. A brawl of madmen whose nerves have been set on edge by the rage of a mob, madmen barking like famished jackals and running . . . running after each other, armed with stones, bottles, clubs, machetes, and old hunks of scrap iron; they run everywhere and nowhere, leaving long reddish-purple trails behind them.

Oh, odious spectacle which costs the life of a human being!

Under the sun of man, a harmless pecking of young chicks sometimes gives birth to an infernal battle of the bulls.

III

PAPA MBOYA'S BLOODTHIRSTY GOAT

(To my friend Zavida whom I no longer recognized when he visited my hut)

Blacken yourself further, Zavida . . . . With coal or tar, it makes no difference! No longer straighten those kinky locks which Mother Nature portioned out to you. Quickly pull out those phony gold teeth which the young women of Yaounde never cease to admire, and make yourself teeth of jet-black onyx.

What . . . ? You resist? You don't seem to understand? Well, listen to the story of Papa Mboya's bloodthirsty goat, and you will see what the desire to offend nature can cost.

In my village, there once lived an honest old peasant who possessed the largest sheep-fold in the area. The children were in the habit of calling him Papa Mboya.

In his eyes, the capricious nation of bleating, gamboling, grass-eating creatures was all that remained in life to entertain a man of his age. It wasn't that Papa Mboya lacked children. He had two of them: twins who, in his company, constituted an admirable trio of look-alikes. But, curiously enough, the old man was less attached to his children than to his animals!

Each day at the first crowing of the cocks, this extraordinary old fellow gets up. His coat, his pipe, his cane: and there he is stationed at the sheep-fold! Greeted by enthusiastic bleatings, he gestures frantically until the blazing sun obliges him to leave the place.

What was he doing there when all the other old men were still wallowing in the arms of sleep? Well, he was delivering a sermon, a long sermon punctuated by animated expressions with a gripping emphasis. He was deploying all his energies to warn his flock against hyenas.

"My children," he repeated, "never leave your homeland. Remember the tragic end of Elcabro, your ancestor, who was eaten by hyenas. . . !"

The sheep were all ears as the old man spoke, and they showed their approval by applauding in their own way.

Yet despite these precautions, the sheep-fold was not completely sheltered from danger. In the early morning, the old peasant harangued his flock, but in the evening, the flock never returned with its numbers intact.

Among the dispirited sheep, however, there was a rather ingenious young he-goat who, from the moment he attained the age of reason, had been meditating on the best way to escape the hyenas' jaws. A white coat with black spots, long horns, a small "Hausa witch-doctor" beard, a mystical gaze — this he-goat was easily recognizable, and he responded to the name of Moambu.

One fine sunny morning young Moambu, defying Papa Mboya's admonitions, ventured about five miles from his native fold. Finding himself at one end of a shaded clearing, he fell into a state of great amazement. There was grass of every variety and color. Wild flowers he'd never before seen or tasted were strewn all around him. Overcome with excitment, Moambu was convinced that he was in a paradise where he was the sole master.

Our little gourmet glanced disdainfully at a bouquet of milky, sweet-smelling *sissongos**. Alas, they were no longer a fitting dish for a goat of his quality! From that moment on, his culinary preferences tilted toward lupines, *politricos*, alfalfa, and the finest species of mushrooms. . . . His eyes, bigger than his belly, incited him to eat everything — roots, suckers, skins, fruits, flowers, leaves. He ate so much that, after his feast, he stretched out in the shade of a palm tree to day-dream while solemnly indulging in the siesta imposed by his well-filled stomach!

"Ah!" he sighed ecstatically. That old fellow Papa Mboya is a crafty devil! Why warn us against such an ideal refuge, far from those bothersome watch-dogs who are always teasing and snarling? Where are all those hyenas he's always telling us about?"

Our naive little adventurer was still grumbling about the good Papa Mboya, when he suddenly found himself nose-to-nose with a sinister figure: it was a hyena!

Tongue hanging out and foaming disgustingly at the mouth, this particular hyena appeared to have been on a strict diet for the past three hundred and thirty-three days!

"Hou-ou-ou!" it howled with obvious satisfaction.

"Prr. . .maah!" bleated Moambu who, sick at heart, had jumped up with a start.

"God be praised for this chance meeting!" cried the hyena, whose eyes were aflame with a murderous appetite.

"Allow me to share the joy inspired by our happy encounter," boldly replied the little goat. "I am Prince Moambu from the sheep-fold of Papa Mboya, of whom you have certainly heard speak. A certain business matter obliges me to go immediately to his majesty, your king . . . . Let us go there together."

What honest and loyal citizen would not tremble with respect at words like "prince" and "his majesty, your king"? No one! It was for this reason that the half-starved hyena was careful not to gobble up Moambu on the spot.

People wouldn't have believed their eyes, if they had run across these two traditional enemies keeping company together so peacefully.

Ah, if Papa Mboya had only been there to see his dear Moambu pass through the virgin forest! If he had only been there to see Moambu escorted by a hyena — to see him,

---

*extremely common West African grass with curving, spiked flower stalks

28

with his own eyes, just two steps from danger — how he would have sobbed with anxiety! How he would have gathered all the dogs in the world into a pack and armed all the best hunters of Nonomotape to save . . . his beloved Moambu!

Be all that as it may, in the country of the hyenas, Moambu's arrival caused every heart to beat a little faster. The king suspended the royal audience to see . . . . Bystanders glanced at each other to see . . . . Young folks moved about in the courtyard to see . . . a living he-goat among hyenas? It's a sight to make all the jaws in the world drop with amazement!

Introduced into the courtyard of His Majesty the King, Moambu experienced a quarter hour that seemed like a season in hell. The audience had resumed, and the bailiff's voice echoed like blows of an air hammer in his ears.

"The hyena condemned to a fine of so many lambs . . . ! That one to so many ewes . . . ! A third to so many he-goats at least six months old . . . !"

Still bloated with succulent delicacies, Moambu's entire belly trembled. And there was indeed good reason to tremble!

"At least six months old! That's my age exactly!" he repeated to himself.

Fines succeeded fines, and all of them were irrevocable!

But what exactly did Moambu want from his majesty, the king of the hyenas? He made it known at the end of the audience, as soon as he had been summoned.

Unfeeling fate! Imagine a little six-month-old he-goat, armed with a pointed beard and two cartilaginous horns, incapable of frightening anyone, in front of an enormous assembly of hyenas. Nevertheless, having collected himself, Moambu declared:

"Excellency, it is I, good prince Moambu from the sheep-fold of Papa Mboya. To contest the supremacy of the hyena nation over the nation of sheep would constitute an unpardonable defiance of divine justice. After long and mature reflection, I have concluded that the best policy is a peaceful coexistence in which all bleating folk voluntarily submit to your noble appetites. I will deliver my fellow countrymen to you, and in so doing, I bring to your exalted attention that they already recognize the honor accorded them when they are being devoured by hyenas! Ah, Sire! The belly of the stronger is the most fitting tomb for all honest weaklings, isn't it?"

These declarations were received with interminable ovations. The king of the hyena nation warmly praised Prince Moambu. He proclaimed him the wisest, most knowledgeable, most brilliant of all the he-goats he had ever seen and . . . devoured. He dressed the young prince in a luxurious hyena skin and proclaimed: "By the power invested in me by God, I solemnly grant you authority over the principality of sheep-folds. And in recognition of your rare heroism, from this time forward you shall be one of us."

The most difficult part of the whole business was that Moambu needed to learn how to howl when necessary. They undertook the task of teaching him the art of howling at the royal school for hyena princes. Yet how painful it was to hear him bawling, barking, braying, croaking, clucking, yelping, cooing, and babbling all day long! Nothing more difficult than a foreign language!

"Hou. . .oo. . .ouououh!" went the professor-hyena.

"Prr. . .maah . . . ou-maah . . . ou-maah ," went the young beginner, sweat welling up from all his pores.

Alternately, his efforts evoked pity and uproarious laughter, for, born a goat, he knew how to bleat delightfully, but nothing in the world could make him howl like a true hyena.

Nevertheless, they pushed on; they hurried things along. The same day Moambu received all the honors of the regimental school, he was, to his great astonishment, elevated to the rank of General of the Army.

Naturally, General Moambu was called upon to play an important role among his new fellow-citizens.

Every day he could be seen leading a pack of hyenas. He spied, he sniffed about, he worked his way through thickets, and he hid himself somewhere not far from his native fold. There, pretending to be in a bad way, he bleated for a long time, sorrowfully, patiently . . . . Then, attracted by these plaintive bleatings, the sheep who came running to save one of their own inevitably fell into the fangs of the hyenas.

Thus, the wisest, most knowledgeable, most brilliant of he-goats returned with his predatory troop to a glorious hail of "bravos" and "hurrahs."

As one can well imagine, that ingenious stratagem bore fruit for several days. Papa Mboya's sheep-fold was visibly losing its population. Finally, it contained no more than ten sheep, ten skeletal sheep reduced to shadows of their former selves by the gust of terror they inhaled each day.

But here's what happened one evening. Papa Mboya had just brought back his unhappy flock. He was contemplating the setting sun as if to confide his misfortunes in it, when suddenly an unwonted bleating arose from a nearby bush. His eyes strained from their sockets, as he rushed headlong toward the suspicious place.

The vigilant old fellow was well aware that his ten surviving sheep had all been present before he barricaded the stalls and closed the gate that evening.

"What luck," he mumbled sadly, "to find an eleventh one! What I need is to see all the others return as a consequence of similar fortunate accidents!"

He had scarcely finished formulating this wish, when he became transfixed as he recognized a ridiculously disguised Moambu fleeing helter-skelter in front of two, three, five, ten . . . oh, in front of an entire battalion of hyenas.

In his honest shepherd's heart, Papa Mboya believed that the hyenas were going to eat his beloved Moambu. Thus, he tried to call him back, as he had done in the past: "Moambu . . . ! Moambu . . . ! Wait . . . ! I'll get the dogs . . . ! I'll get the dogs, and I'll arm myself to save you . . . !"

Nonsense! To the devil with packs of dogs and weapons; Moambu wants nothing to do with them, poor old Papa Mboya!

As a result of turning this event over and over in his memory, the good peasant finally understood that the goat, whose fate had so tormented him, was actually the author of his misfortune. Rather than wasting his time in futile lamentations, he chose to apply the surest means of protecting the dear remaining members of his flock.

You must know that, being in the vanguard of his pillaging band, Moambu was compelled by civic duty to return the next day and the next . . . . Crouching as usual in a heavily wooded thicket, he bleated, he moaned: silence! He whined, he uttered a death-rattle: no one! From that moment on, the stratagem proved ineffective. From that moment on, there were also no more "bravos" or "hurrahs" for General Moambu. After many fruitless hunting parties, the hyenas, who had become accustomed to good food, began to lose weight.

First, you no longer heard anyone speak about a friend of the hyena-nation: then, the foreigner was designated a "stateless person." Finally, there were disquieting looks, whisperings, and rumors which allowed no room for equivocation. Everywhere it was proclaimed that one should finally settle accounts with the gallows-bird who was causing such a nation-wide famine!

Without further ado, the wisest, most knowledgeable, most brilliant goat in the world experienced the macabre joy of being eaten by an entire nation of hyenas who had been howling with hunger all day long.

Blacken yourself further, Zavida, and make yourself teeth of jet-black onyx. No longer straighten those kinky locks which Mother Nature portioned out to you.

IV

AT THE YAOUNDE CENTRAL POST OFFICE

"Your presence is requested at the post office!" my friend Louis Ongolo announced to me that day.

At these words, an icy shiver ran down my spine. For a long time I had not breathed the air of the city center. My heart filled with bitterness and anguish as I thought of all the turmoil I would have to confront. Mounted aboard my "Commer,"* I departed . . . .

The throbbing of an airplane skimming the treetops. The wheezing of an old rattletrap that was smoking, spitting, and dawdling along. The swarming of pedestrians who allow one to pass only with great difficulty . . . ! My nerves were frayed.

The Cathedral square imposes an unpleasant halt on us all, as we find ourselves entangled in an endless line of vehicles waiting for permission to proceed.

Truly, above and beyond coincidence, the name "Brouillet" is quite well suited for such a noisy corner.** From morning to evening, the constant bustle admits no truce. The crackling farts of motorcycles, the blasts of car horns, the coming and going of bicyclists and pedestrians only serve to accentuate the intermittent traffic jams which block the street. A sight to take away the breath of a rustic fellow fresh from his native forest!

Nearby, the railroad crossing gates open and close again. With the serenity of an enormous lady-bug, the locomotive passes slowly and emits a whistle capable of breaking your eardrums. Clusters of eucalyptus trees are roused to anger by this din, and in their superannuated immobility, they brandish their powerless arms furiously, as if to beg the heavens for calm and peace.

All alone, in the midst of this agitation, the Mfoundi River silently drains its waters beneath the bridge — waters strewn with rubbish . . . and with mysteries. Over there somewhere, the Treasury building is hidden, like a scrupulous old miser, behind a high masonry wall. From its peaceful entrenchment, it spies upon the enormous mass of

---

* a self-propelled vehicle invented by the handicapped author
**the French name "Brouillet" suggests confusion or quarrelling

concrete which comprises the sole post office in the city of Yaounde.

This post office was born, they say, at the same time as World War II. It even has the air of desiring to shout at every passerby: "I symbolize one of the greatest sacrifices which Cameroon, under French mandate, willingly accepted during a period of economic crisis."

In any case, it belongs to that category of structures in which the Cameroonian capital can justly take pride.

Modern in style, this building, which has no more than a single floor, stands proudly at the corner and even invades a large part of the intersection. Irregular in form, its broad facade terminates in an arc. Resting solidly on a thick subfoundation, its high walls contain small bull's-eye windows with bars. Inscribed in raised black characters like the tattoo of a secret clan, the portal bears three letters: "P.T.T."

At the sight of these three letters, a memory flits across my mind.

I was still quite small. One day my father took me for a walk in the city. We were passing near the "Brouillet" intersection, when he asked me if I didn't want to become a postal worker after I had finished my studies . . . . With the candid seriousness one sometimes encounters in children, I drew an admiring glance from him with the retort: "No father! You see, those three letters 'P.T.T.' really mean 'Perds Ton Temps'!"*

The Yaounde Post Office has always evoked in me that tender memory; how long ago it was!

Its roof is a sort of platform which contrasts sharply with the vulgar, slanting ridges of the other buildings in the neighborhood. The public penetrates into the main floor of the post office not only by means of two small side doors, but also through a large central portal which, when closed, sports a highly respectable iron gate.

The service windows are arranged in one long, spacious room. An abundant daylight enters through windows of diverse colors; no one would be inconvenienced by darkness in this place. Comfort is hardly lacking: telephone booths and telephone books remain wide open to serve the world of affairs.

But what confusion inside the building!

Calmly installed behind their windows, employees serve the customers as soon as they present themselves. The floor, covered with tiles, groans daily beneath countless leather soles. The architectural majesty of this building seems to impose a polite silence upon a numerous and varied clientele. Blacks and whites, city-dwellers and peasants come together here without jostling each other. A living model of all races and social classes for whom peaceful coexistence remains a real possibility.

Outside near the entrance, a continuous hubbub rises and falls. The steps of the enormous staircase are being stormed from all directions. Swarms of men and women. Newspaper salesmen harassing passersby. Carts with display stands lined up on the sidewalk beneath the calculating eyes of rogues shouting at the top of their lungs: "Smoke Bastos . . . I Drink Beaufort . . . !"

---

*P.T.T. is an abbreviation for Post Office (in French: "Postes, Téléphones, Télécommunications."). "Perds ton temps" is the equivalent of "Waste your time."

Besides this incongruous crowd, attracted and held there until the fall of evening by an unforeseen clientele, the place crawls with idle onlookers. Leisurely resting their elbows on the iron guard-rails, they mockingly censure passing pedestrians and vehicles, exchange bits of local gossip, and watch the endless film of street scenes.

Let us not forget, alas, the lepers, the cripples, the blind, the victims of sleeping sickness. Their names obliterated in that hell of harsh noises, this vulgar folk begs alms from every passing face, while tirelessly improvising interminable songs of sorrow.

Business finished, I would have liked my little car to carry me back as quickly as a *sputnik* . . .! And, wrapped in thought, I continued to puzzle over that bewildering riddle which is human society: inevitable meeting place of those who laugh and those who weep. . . .

V

MANDARI, A FIFTY-YEAR OLD DEMOISELLE

Very early one morning about two months after my arrival in Nlong Kak, a dreadful racket jarred me from my slumbers.

"You've got to clear out, clear out this very day . . . ! You're trying my patience to the utmost. . . ! Here it is four months that you haven't paid any rent. And you tell me to wait. Wait for what?"

I recognized the voice of my landlord, who had flared up at some insolvent tenant.

"Clear out this very day . . . ! As it is, I have accorded you as much respect as a respectable main can pay to respectable woman . . . !"

"Not so loud!" the woman pleaded in a pitiful tone of voice. "You know I'm not working. You know that my sole means of subsistence is brewing and selling *harki!** You yourself have seen the stagnation recently experienced in that line of business! Corn too expensive! Distillery working poorly! And this neighborhood swarming with dishonest customers! Why do you doubt my good faith . . . ?"

"No, no, and once again no!" thundered the man. "I don't give a damn for your line of business! Illegal sector, furthermore! If you can't pay your rent, any attempt to make me feel sorry for you with such idle tales will be utterly useless. . . ! My house—get it into hour head once and for all—will never be turned into a charitable institution! You're trying my patience to the utmost. I'm tell you! You've got to clear out this very day . . . !"

"Not so loud!" the poor woman repeated obstinately. "One last time, I beg of you, sir, be patient for just one more week. . . ."

This final word had hardly been pronounced when a sudden barrage of sound gave me a disagreeable start. A crystalline sound of breaking glasses and bottles; a silvery sound of dishes and kitchen utensils; a dull sound of old crates splintering, of empty chests and barrels being dashed against the wall. I understood.

The exasperated landlord has remained silent in order to indulge himself in acts of brutality under the stupefied gaze of the woman who stood powerlessly by and watched

---

*local corn beer

him going about his business.

I was unable to fall back asleep, since the racket continued to mount until it threatened to bring down the entire house. I was obliged to go out and install myself in my accustomed place.

Various objects were scattered about the porch floor. What particularly attracted my attention was a picture portraying the naked, intertwined bodies of a white man and a black woman, both laughing blissfully. This pornographic document reposed in the mud, surrounded by handkerchiefs, scarves, panties, combs, bras, napkins, dish towels, and old letters . . . .One could also make out flasks of all shapes and colors. And on top of all these intimate baubles was fiercely enthroned a wash basin filled with young ears of corn — the principal ingredient in the production of *harki*.

The landlord had already left, railing at his wretched tenant. I remained wrapt in thought before this spectacle, struggling to repress the compassionate impulses which weighed upon my heart. Desirous of escaping from this internal conflict, I resolved to embark with Candide and Pangloss for Lisbon! Alas, I had the misfortune of being unable to immediately savor the delights of this marvelous voyage. . . .

*

*   *

"Good morning, Monsieur!" a voice broken with sorrow called out to me.

Astonished, I raise my head, and in front of me I see a woman amiably extending her hand toward me. She greets me and goes over to lean against the wall.

She was a woman about fifty years old and possessed of a natural beauty. Muffled in an ample frock and wrapped in a native cloth with blue flowers on a white background, she was of average height and had a light complexion. Her hair was extremely black, and it descended across the back of her neck in long, voluptuous tresses. Two large alluring eyes brightly lighted her broad face from beneath well-covered brow ridges. But this quite pretty face bore the mark of advanced age and past sufferings. Her look sparkled with intelligence and announced a light-hearted spirit. Her nose was delicate; her mouth was small and sensual. The corners of her lips looked as if they had been daubed with *pinari*, a black cosmetic powder with which Moslem women paint their eyes. Copper and ivory bracelets clacked in annoyance on her weak little wrists. Rings with large stones and engraved with the signs of the zodiac comprised a veritable arsenal of self-defense on her slender, well taloned fingers. She had all the qualities of an Oriental woman and gave off the same strong perfume which emanates from "public women."

First, she stared at me for a while, as an engaging smile wandered across her face. Then, without raising her voice, she said to me in pidgin: "Probably the gentleman is bored, *like me*, in this section of town where everything makes one feel so blue."

"Me? Why should I be bored, Madame?" I asked in surprise.

"*Mademoiselle!*" she corrected shyly. "It's true that one has the right to be bored here. This monotonous silence is suited to wearing out someone with a high-flying spirit. Modern man could easily become 'de-civilized' in such a sad and narrow setting!"

"Just the opposite is true," I told her. "This out-of-the-way neighborhood is the best of refuges for an enterprising man. Tormented all day long by harsh and unpleasant noises, elderly city-dwellers would do well to come here each evening for a walk."

The woman coughed, breathed deeply, and continued with a confident air, "Monsieur, ever since I moved into this calm, to which you apparently attach such value, I feel worn out, as if I were carrying about some mysterious illness. You've only just arrived. May heaven spare you the disgusting sensation which I feel. You have the stuff to be a person of good company, and such a gloomy environment hardly suits you . . . ."

"Oh . . . ! Why not?"

"Because . . . !" she tossed out, with the faint smile of someone who desires to compel an interlocutor's favorable response. "After seeing you for such a short time, I ask myself under what skies we may have met for the first time. . . ."

"That's just what I was asking myself, Madame, as I was looking at you."

"Mademoiselle!" the woman corrected me once again. Then she continued in the most unconstrained tone, "I didn't have the pleasure, as far as I know, of having lived with you anywhere. But as far back as my memories go, I'm convinced that somewhere — I don't know where — I met a young man who resembles you like a twin brother."

I sighed, and the woman asked me if I hadn't lived in Kribi, Douala, Dizangué, Fernando Po, Manoko, Victoria, Nkongsamba. . . . As I shook my head, she burst out, "Not even in Ntui?"

"In Ntui? Yes, but only passing through, Madame!"

"If that is so, didn't you ever hear of a certain Mandari, connoisseur of dancing, princess of Yoko, idol of the colonial administrators of the period . . . ? Well, that's me in the flesh!" she said proudly, as if she had just made a heroic revelation.

Then, with a captivating talkativeness, Mandari, connoisseur of dancing, princess of Yoko, idol of the colonial administrators of the period, led me through the labyrinth of her past . . . .

"I was born in the village of Mankim," she said, "six years before the Germans were obliged to withdraw from Cameroon. The favorite daughter in a large family, I was blessed with a beauty of which everyone sung praises. Although happy, I was dismayed by the fact that I couldn't admire myself in a mirror, an object unknown at that time in my part of the country. Peacefully, I grew up in the paternal sare,* far from the rough work of the fields. Stretched out all day long on a mat at my father's feet, I had only to eat well and sleep soundly, being but rarely occupied in relighting his pipe with a live coal.

"My eleventh birthday arrived accompanied by an onslaught of marriage proposals. Sheep, cattle, and horses were not the only goods offered to my father as payment for my dowry. Certain princes who wanted desperately to win my hand put weapons and slaves on display. But every suitor was irrevocably checked by the

---

*Among the Fulani of the Savannah, the sare is a group of houses owned by one family and fenced around by high walls.

obstinacy of my father, who always gave another girl in my place.

"Seven years later, a mysterious illness struck my beloved father. For two weeks, the best witch-doctors vied with death for his soul, but all in vain! With a profound respect for the dead man's last wish, the council of elders passed the ruler's staff to the young girl that I was then.

"Ah! You should have seen me at the moment of my ascension to the throne. I cry, I refuse, I struggle, I veil my face . . . . All the old women of Mankim rise up against me. . . .

"In spite of myself, I ruled for five years at Mankim. And during that thorny period, I did everything in my power to acquire all the virtues demanded by my civic duty, but to no avail. To tell the truth, there is no heavier or more awkward burden than governing a society. Scold, threaten, and the people take you for a miserable dictator. Advise, smile at everybody, and the very same people accuse you of lacking authority. To be a good leader, it's doubtless necessary to be angel and devil at the same time.

"However naive and childish my proposed resolutions might have been, they were always greeted with enthusiastic approval by my subjects. The traditional story-tellers covered me with endless litanies of praise, comparing me to the Dawn, to the Shepherd's Star, to the Full Moon . . . . But in the end, nothing could dislodge my shyness. The simple glance of a man exercised an irresistable influence over my soul. Ah! Men! Their eyes are so often full of diabolical sparks.

"Being unable to take any more, I abdicated the ruler's staff, preferring to throw myself into the arms of freedom and adventure. What joys and ambushes awaited me in that obscure Bohemian existence? Only God knew. As for me, I merely knew that I possessed a precious treasure — beauty — which, if skillfully exploited, opens doors to enviable situations for many women. Convinced from the beginning that fortune would smile upon me if I became a prostitute, I lost no time in becoming the sad *Madelon** of the military camps in Ntui and Batchenga, where all the foreigners who had resisted General De Gaulle's call to arms were being interned. But soon after, harrassed by the local authorities, I went to Obala, where one of my second cousins was working in a trading house.

"It was there that I became the beloved mistress of a Greek merchant. Two years later, this white man offers to formalize the legal status of our conjugal relationship. I refuse, alleging that, according to my father's dying wish, I would die if I took a husband. In actual fact, that was no more than an evasive tactic, for I had really hoped to become the wife of a black man. Of a sufficiently well educated black man occupying a situation founded on a comfortable fortune. However, as they say 'Man proposes and God disposes!' Heaven refused me a husband of my taste . . . .

"The war over, my Greek returned for good to his native country. He entrusted me

---

*A corruption of "Magdalene." According to French military usage, a "Madelon" was a woman who entertained officers and soldiers in a bar. By extension, it became a euphemism for "prostitute."

to one of his countrymen, who was also a merchant. But within a year, I had to leave my new spouse. Getting drunk every evening, this second Greek threatened to electrocute me one night, because I objected to certain sexual bestialities unknown to our customs. In his company, I for the first time heard a man deny the existence of God! In his company, I understood that all white men were not civilized, regardless of what most blacks think! And, remembering everything that white man asked me to do, I ask myself sometime if blacks alone don't deserve to enter the House of God . . . !

"After having fraudulently amassed many possessions in the house of this Greek, I fled and went to Edea, Douala, Kribi, Fernando Po. I even tried my hand at Spanish Guinea and British Cameroon. Three years later I arrived in Yaounde, where, endowed with talent and grace, I became a tango and *assiko** dancer capable of fluttering all the hearts in the city.

"Alas, I fell under the domination of a student who beguiled me with fickle, indefinite plans of marriage and then abandoned me after having ruined me. That's how a man returns a woman's kindness! Thus, I swore that from then on I would remain eternally ungrateful toward the entire race of men . . . !

"Admirable and beautiful star in the brightest circles of Yaounde, I experienced a new phase of my existence beginning in 1950. Lamentable phase, to be sure! As a matter of fact, my admirers became fewer and less enthusiastic. Finally, they disappeared altogether . . . . And, in spite of redoubled beauty treatments, time mercilessly spread the indelible cream of middle age across my face.

"I was obliged to bow to affliction and I succeeded rather poorly in getting out of that scrape. Born to affluence, raised in comfortable circumstances and having flourished in indolence, I struggled desperately against manual labor, which seemed like an unbreakable rock to me.

"At that time, prostitution once again stretched its broad and horrible arms toward me. Ah, Monsieur. . . ! Do you know what a whore is? Well, imagine a human rag, repudiated by honest folk and cursed by the heavens — running about the city and the world, conscience rotten to the core and practically extinguished, stomach empty and body steeped in strange odors — delighting in debauchery, abandoning itself in every embrace, dragging immorality about like a treasure chest and all for the sole reward of falling into misery and infamy after a day of devilishly hard work."

Mandari paused, breathing heavily, as if she had just climbed a steep hill. Then with a certain liveliness, she continued, "However, as for me, I was a high-class prostitute. All Yaounde spoke of no one but me in the dance-halls and the government offices. Beautiful, serious, and proud, I introduced discord in many a household, I bewitched civil servants, administrators, military officers, parliamentarians, and even ministers of the church. . . !"

"Aie-aie-aieee . . . !" I exclaimed dumbfounded.

This woman of the world had spontaneously confided her singular accomplish-

---

*An African dance usually accompanied by guitar music.

ment to me as if she had just discovered a balm to console her for the outrage which her landlord had inflicted on her.

"What is it then?" she went on. "To judge by the astonishment I read on your face, I have the impression that you are but a poor novice in this chapter of life! You don't know then, Monsieur, what exploits a beautiful woman is capable of bringing about in the realm of love! And what a woman . . . ! Me . . . ! Me. . . Mandari, whose charms had become proverbial. Yes, even ministers of the church! Priests, not to speak of catechists . . . ! And I swear it on the grave of my father!"

"*Bidim!* . . ." I exclaimed again, distracted. "That's too much swearing, Madame! I'm not disagreeing with you."

It was quite inadvertantly that I again pronounced the word, "Madame," and then only under the influence of a shameful revelation. Until then, I had been unable to consider the epithet "Mademoiselle" as an appropriate title for such an elderly trollop. And I was mistaken in thinking she wouldn't pay much attention to it.

"That name again!" she interrupted with an arrogance intended as familiarity. "How infatuated you are with that pretty little word, 'Madame'!"

"I humbly beg your pardon, Ma-de-moi-selle," I said, carefully articulating each syllable.

Immediately, I discerned a humiliated smile crease the folds at the corners of the old woman's eyes. She looked me up and down, pensively shook her head, then expressed this thought: "Excuse me, Monsieur. . .! All the time I see you with your eyes buried in books. You ought to know the meaning of the word 'Madame' better than I do. I have reason to believe that it is the noble title of a married woman. . . !"

"That's true, Mad. . ." I was unable to finish, because my throat had become filled with saliva, and I had begun to cough painfully.

"At this very moment some dear creature is probably dreaming about Monsieur," she said. "That's according to the superstitions in my part of the country. But that dear creature — I hope it's not a beautiful abandoned woman like me, perchance! Poor her, and poor me . . . !"

During her long confession, she had been distractedly surveying the road and, from time to time, staring at me. Suddenly, she sat down on the porch floor, and Mandari no longer held back tears and sobs.

"Poor me!" she groaned, covering her eyes. "Is this what Providence has been reserving for me in life?"

Then Mandari remained silent for a moment, as if an internal voice had suddenly revealed that tears reduce one's human dignity. Nevertheless she began again, and with even greater force, "Oh! the good old days. . . ! Fields of corn and groundnuts, rice paddies where just before the harvest the children all perched on the observation towers and joyously ran after the birds. . . . ! And barns brimming with harvested crops and storerooms filled with the scent of honey . . . !

"Oh! the good old days . . . ! White men who adored me! Soft beds! Solid brick houses! Tables covered with gourmet delights! A kitchen swarming with scullery boys, washerwomen, workers who respectfully quarreled over the honor of serving me . . . !

40

"Oh! the good old days . . . ! Disappointed suitors who wept out of spite and knelt down before me . . . !

"Oh! the good old days . . . ! Poor me . . . ! Me who had nothing more to do than to eat well and sleep soundly . . . ! Me who held the keys to well-filled strong-boxes and governed all the domestic expenses of a white man . . . ! Here I am today being chased from a dirty hovel like this for not having paid an insignificant little rent. . . !

"Oh! poor me . . . ! No father, no mother, no husband, no children . . . ! And here I am condemned to live miserably in the garbage heap of society . . . !"

Poor Mandari's face, smooth and serene a few moments ago, suddenly appeared to be scored with deep wrinkles. I understood why: her tears had washed away her make-up. The indiscreet but fatal traces of harsh Time — that cruel and invincible god — presented themselves in their true light.

This old demoiselle, idol of an age, sobbed and tirelessly poured forth her Jeremiads.

Something touched my heart; something like an icy vapor, a heavy blast of air, a magnetized fluid, something which inflicted on me an unpleasant shuddering at the sight of those bitter tears which fell, which fell abundantly, which fell ceaselessly from the eyes of a suffering human being.

"Mademoiselle, life is like that!" I said, hoping to console her.

In fact, at these words, Mandari, unhappy Mandari, suddenly became silent, wiped her tears and smiled at me. . . .

I understood what a magical effect can be produced in the heart of a fifty-year-old spinster by the simple word "Mademoiselle," when it is pronounced with a touch of devotion.

VI

THE DOG AND THE CHIMPANZEE

That morning, the small market place was more animated than usual. A salvo of uproarious laughter crackled intermittantly from a crowd gathered in front of a man who, with a distant look in his eye, was seated in a corner next to two small animals. . . .

"Massa, you like?" he inquired after having measured me from head to foot with his gaze. "A thousand francs* for the little dog, and a thousand five hundred for the little chimpanzee. Massa, please . . . ! It's to pay my taxes."

A raucous outcry arose at these words.

"No! No. . . ! Sell a dog and a chimpanzee at the same time! Cursed be anyone who gives his money!" they exclaimed from all sides.

I didn't understand their objections. Disturbed by my equivocal attitude in front of the man who was selling the dog and the chimpanzee, a stranger took me aside and advised me against buying the two small creatures.

"It's dangerous!" he confided in me.

"Because?"

"Our ancestors, who were not crazy, believed it to be so. And here is the origin of their belief:

One day, having left their native forest, Dog and Chimpanzee went to the city of Men to seek an advantageous marriage.

Along the way, they engaged in long conversations like those one hears from the most audacious rakes and adventurers. Entirely devoted to succeeding in the amorous conquests they had planned, they trudged along, eyes scintillating with joy and heads filled with lofty schemes. There was a briskness in their steps, and they stopped at every turning of the road to say fine things to each other, to laugh uproariously, to embrace each other fraternally . . . .

Suddenly, recalling some disconcerting thought, the dog said to the chimpanzee: "Comrade, here we are a stone's throw from the city of Men. Are we courting a misfortune that could justify all the racial prejudices directed against us? I hope that,

---

*approximately four dollars

like me, you haven't the slightest desire for that, comrade!"

"Now there's something that's well put!" returned the other. "But what should we do, comrade, to avoid a dishonorable outcome and prove to Men that we are not common insignificant creatures?"

"As for me, revealed the dog, "munching on bones is a congenital mania which nothing in the world could cure. Although sacred to my race, this custom disgusts the race of men. And only a practical joker would pretend ignorance of the fact. I take pleasure in believing, comrade, that you are a sincere friend, a friend who wishes me well, a friend who would not think of throwing a bone on the ground at the risk of disgracing me in front of men."

As he listened to this wise discourse, the gallant chimpanzee was thunderstruck. "Aha!" he uttered, astonished. "My father was certainly right, for when he was still alive, he told me that dogs were the most intelligent race in the world. Your wonderful initiative confirms his wisdom for me today. Here I am now forewarned against any rash action which might compromise our engagements . . . . Well, since confidence should be reciprocal, I will no longer hide from you, comrade, the fact that Mother Nature did a very sketchy job on my buttocks. In depriving me of my clothes, one could turn me into a laughing-stock for all men."

"Indeed," continued the dog, "let us do everything to pass in men's eyes for suitors adorned from head to toe with noble qualities."

"Yes," chorused the chimpanzee, "let us do everything to sustain the honor of our two nations among men."

In their excitement, both of them emitted an ear-splitting peal of laughter. Once these confidences had been exchanged, the dog and the chimpanzee continued on their way and arrived at their destination a little before sunset.

The two financées-to-be made no secret of their joy at seeing the two suitors attired in their Sunday best and coming from such fabulous, far-away places. As quick as a wink, they prepared the "meal for strangers." It was one of those meals which exudes the most tempting odors and which is reserved by traditional custom for only the most important guests.

After allowing themselves to be solicited at some length by the prospective in-laws, the suitors installed themselves in front of plates filled with food. Each, naturally, elbow-to-elbow with his betrothed.

History will doubtless never record another assembly quite like this one. The atmosphere was absolutely perfect, and under the circumstances, exceptionally harmonious. At each mouthful, kisses and words of endearment succeeded each other endlessly. And the whole scene was punctuated with periodic outbursts of laughter.

Nevertheless, in this idyllic circle, not everyone could avoid losing his head. Thus it was that Master Chimpanzee grabbed a fine-looking mutton bone and threw it far from the table, very far from the table and into the village square. Immediately, the laughter ceased.

Mechanically, the dog in a single bound leaped upon the indigestible morsel. Completely flabbergasted, the men looked at each other and heaped mockeries upon

43

the dog. They cried shame; they insulted the strange suitor who had such grotesque manners. Comrade Dog silently endured the irrevocable disappointment of his hopes.

Far from sympathizing with his friend's misfortune, Master Chimpanzee associated himself with the jeering crowd. He began to laugh with the two prospective fiancees and the villagers. He began to roar with laughter, his eyes filling with tears! And the idea of obtaining both women of Men for himself alone was already revolving in his ambitious brain.

But as night resolutely covered the city with its mysterious mantel . . . .

While Master Chimpanzee triumphed and dreamed contentedly in a soft bed, Comrade Dog, despised by everyone and tormented by vexation, was flinging himself about on the hard ground, unable to close his eyes.

Early in the morning, he woke up with the partridges. Little by little, the village too woke up, whereas the snoring of Master Chimpanzee, still sleeping like a child, continued to resound with ever-increasing volume.

"Ah yes!" muttered Comrade Dog ironically in front of the men, "sleeping late is indeed the lot of a fortunate lover!"

And in order not to disturb this well-deserved snooze, prospective fathers-in-law, mothers-in-law, brothers-in-law, sisters-in-law, in short, all the in-laws, spared no pains.

As far as the "Eye of the Heavens" was concerned, it was a bit inclined toward mockery during this grandiose ceremony and darted its softest rays of light through holes in the side of the hut and onto this sleeping fellow.

But nothing can last forever! Thus, the snoring of Master Chimpanzee ultimately stopped. Finally awake, he glanced about. He rubbed his eyes to see better. . . . Alas, he saw no more than a disconcertingly empty space. . . . Impossible! At first he thought it must be an inconsequential dream. Oh, harsh reality! His clothes . . . . Where were his clothes? He came to the realization that he had been the victim of a highly successful act of revenge. In the calm of the night, the dog had hurriedly made off with his perfidious companion's clothes while muttering, "it's your turn to drink *metet*!"*

The dog had made off with his deceitful companion's clothes and buried them in a latrine-pit behind the hut.

For a moment despair immobilized Master Chimpanzee in his bed. But soon an immense outcry invaded the city of Men. People clapped their hands, they ran, they shouted in unison:

> A ma'nna . . . ooo!
> Eyen, eyen . . . ééé, eyen!
> Mob abed adze!
> Eyen, eyen . . . ééé, eyen!
> Zut ene nye ya?
> Eyen, eyen . . . ééé, eyen!

*a plant with very bitter leaves

Ye benga ba aven?
Eyen, eyen . . . ééé, eyen!
A ma'nna . . . ooo!
Eyen, eyen . . . ééé eyen!
Mob abed adze!
Eyen, eyen . . . ééé, eyen!

O son of my mother!
Marvelous, marvelous, oh marvelous!
How ugly this fellow is!
Marvelous, marvelous, oh marvelous!
What's wrong with his buttocks?
Marvelous, marvelous, oh marvelous!

It might be called an open wound!
Marvelous, marvelous, oh marvelous!
Oh son of my mother!
Marvelous, marvelous, oh marvelous!
How ugly this fellow is!
Marvelous, marvelous, oh marvelous!

Pushing his way through an opening in the corner of the hut, the unfortunate chimpanzee fled toward his native forest, exposing to the jeering of scandalized men the buttocks on which Mother Nature had done such a sketchy job. He was naked, completely naked, although he was amply covered with shame . . . ! He disappeared into his native forest and vowed he would cast an evil spell on anyone who took it into his head to make him live with Dog, the author of his resounding disgrace!

In turn, Master Dog laughed . . . ! He roared with laughter, his eyes filling with tears. And as a result of laughing he lost the use of speech. From that day forward, he could do no more than bark. Still, preferring him to the chimpanzee, the men gave him the hand of both fiancees. And that's the reason why the dog is woman's best companion in our country.

Nevertheless, Master Dog was hardly willing to give up bones, for one can cure an illness but not a hereditary deficiency . . . .

*
*   *

After having listened attentively to my story-teller, I repeated to myself the adage I had learned at the white man's school: "He who laughs last laughs best."

VII

THE LITTLE PHANTOM-CAT

I will never forget that night . . . .

My tormented soul was enjoying a profound repose, when I was suddenly overwhelmed by a strange dream: "Little children were romping around me and amusing themselves by piercing my body with inkpens. The boldest of them succeeded in inflicting me with such a painful wound that I cried out in distress and awoke with a start!"

No, it wasn't an empty dream, but a vision! By the time I had relighted the lantern, my mother was already at my bedside to inquire about what had happened to me. Guided by a sharp pain, I discovered that my thumb was red with blood.

"It's mice!" burst out my mother furiously.

She was not mistaken. I had already noticed that my room was infested with mice. Local superstition contends that those mice were not natural mice; it willingly accords them a human soul and considers them as a legion of totemic creatures in the service of some evil genius or other!

And yet, the simple truth is perhaps that, not having found a sufficient pittance that night, my shameless parasites had blamed their hunger on me and delegated the most famished among them to attack me personally.

Although the bite I had received was a small one, it hurt atrociously. A child would have cried. Satisfied with this bloodthirsty exploit, my bold aggressors must have been huddling together in their hiding place, peacefully intoning their victory hymns. Perhaps they were railing against the vigilance of my mother, who was just now completing her treatment of my injured thumb. But as I was falling asleep in the enchantment of her loving care, she began to grumble between her teeth. What was she saying . . . ? She was cursing the nation of mice! Oh Noble Lady! Motherly love sometimes has its angry passions . . . !

The next morning when I awoke, my first idea was to examine the wound. It had closed almost entirely, and it hurt me less than before. But seeing it again, I felt my heart boiling with disgust for those mice. Scrupulously distrustful, I refused to move my hand anywhere unless it had been preceded by a searching glance. . . .

I desire to pick up my toothbrush, when I perceive with a start that there is something unusual on the table. Frightened, I look; I open my eyes wide to assure myself it's no longer a question of mice! It's a kitten dozing in the warmth of a shoe. Pleasant surprise . . . ! I amuse myself by patting him on the back. Without being troubled by that unexpected caress, he raises his round head in an insolent gesture. He is only a little surprised, like a peaceful tenant who is being bothered by a tactless landlord.

"Miaow, miaow . . . !" he declares, as he directs a questioning glance in my direction.

Where did he come from? Who does he belong to? I haven't the slightest idea.

But how pretty he was, this strange little cat! How pretty he was in his silky white coat with mauve stripes, with his pink nose, his delicate ears with bevelled edges, and his large lustrous eyes . . . ! How pretty he was, this tomcat with a little muzzle that allowed one to glimpse a row of milk-white, chisel-like teeth whenever he meowed! Frail, velvety, scrupulously clean paws, concealing still-harmless claws.

His meowing moved me and solicited my hospitality. A swarm of ideas germinated in my memory. I thought about all those sickly orphans who wander desperately from threshold to threshold on the lookout for any sort of asylum. My heart quivered with pity.

This pretty little cat hadn't yet been weaned. He must have gone astray in the area during an expedition far from his mother. At my side, he found all the sympathy he could have desired. Thus, he didn't need much time to get over that crisis of adjustment which always darkens the stranger's face when he enters someone else's house for the first time.

Overwhelmed with paternal tenderness, he no longer wanted to leave me. I sit down; he sits down beside me. I get up; he gets up and trots along behind me. When I write, he bounds nimbly onto the table and lies down in front of me. There, wagging his small round head and occasionaly twitching his ears or his little feline nose, he follows with a curious eye the bizarre maneuvers of my pen on the the sheet of paper.

At mealtime, he patiently waited beneath the table for his portion. It was wonderful to see him eat the morsel I threw him! For him, it was a point of honor to maintain his fur in an impeccable state. If defiled by an oil stain, a mud spot or a drop of water, it was soon licked clean by dainty thrusts of the tongue.

This little cat had become like a living jewel which adorned my hut and brightened my leisure hours. We forgot ourselves in long games with a mirror: I would pass a mirror in front of him . . . . Ah, you should have seen my young protegé when confronted by his own image! You should have seen him making faces, brandishing one paw and then the other, tilting his head, clawing the smooth surface and, tired of the game, staring at me as if to implore my assistance! In each of his gestures, there was always something which made me smile with a fond compassion!

Young Prosper Nkolo liked to tease him so much! He dragged him by the paws or squeezed his sides, when he wasn't plunging him into a washbasin full of water. But the child liked best of all to pick him up by the neck and shout to passersby at the top of his lungs. "A dead cat!"

As a matter of fact, when Minou was in this position, he no longer moved. He appeared to be anesthetized. As soon as he was released, he ran to me and stared at Nkolo with a murderous glint in his eyes.

It was doubtless because of these childish tyrannies that the little cat insisted on passing the night in my bed. He made his berth on my feet and slept. Touched by this mysterious attachment, I took great pains to avoid disturbing his gentle sleep. And why should I do that? He wasn't like a puppy — filthy, disorderly, and foul-smelling . . . !

We lived in this pleasant state of intimacy for thirty days. And during those thirty days, the mice became scarce in my hut. It wasn't that Minou made war on them! Fresh from his mother's milk, he was unable to engage in that kind of sport! Weak and naive, Minou was actually afraid of mice. But the faint-hearted mice were also very much afraid of Minou. . . !

Here we are on the eve of Easter and the rain is falling in torrents.

Really, it's distressing that a kitten can catch cold so easily! "Mine" began to shiver. At first I thought this fit of fever would pass with the midday sun. But at noon he didn't eat a thing, because he was incapable of holding down the smallest mouthful. He was shaking all over. He could hardly walk any longer; he meowed without pause, staring at me with dying looks. Each meow pierced my heart like a surgeon's scalpel. For a long time, I was paralyzed with anguish and sorrow.

"He is certainly ill!" said young Nkolo from time to time, having become less of a tease with respect to the kitten.

There was nothing more painful than to see that little cat in agony. He insisted on sleeping his last sleep in my bed, but his feeble jumps would not allow him to reach his goal. I who had not the slightest desire to see him die — I invented a thousand expedients to save him. I would have done everything, given everything, to have succeeded.

At one time, I advised the child to cover the dying creature with an old sack. At another, I made the kitten drink a little warm water and quinine. At still another, I (as a practical doctor) prescribed a sun-bath and a fumigation. For a moment, I saw the little cat showing signs of improvement . . . . But about six o'clock in the evening, the child, who was watching over it minute by minute, came running to tell me in a breathless voice: "Papa, our little cat is no longer moving, and his paws have become all stiff! He must be sleeping a very deep sleep! Perhaps he'll wake up healthy!"

"Let's hope so!" I muttered as I left the room.

Nkolo's announcement literally staggered me. I drove every gloomy hypothesis out of my head; I ardently wished for the recovery of my poor tomcat . . . .

Alas! His eyes half closed, his paws immobile and rigid, the little cat was no longer anything but a ball of cotton lying poignantly motionless in the gutter. That motionlessness which disconcerts the Muse of the poets, which commands respect from the genius of scholars and against which every royal sceptre is powerless.

"It was a phantom-cat sent by Providence into your hut, and it was the mice who cast an evil spell on him!" said my mother in a superstitious, melancholy voice.

But me, I lost my good spirits and became motionless before the remains of this young companion of my solitary hours. Night fell on the city. My eyes dimmed with tears. I looked by accident at the sun which was progressively being extinguished on the horizon.

VIII

WHEN THE PUPILS' PARENTS INTERVENE

Among the good souls who sometimes came to enliven my hovel with their human warmth, there was a young teacher, the headmaster of a small school in the neighborhood. When he arrived that afternoon, however, he didn't reply to my greeting with his customary enthusiasm. He sat down on a chair; he coughed several times and put on the hint of a smile. But this smile hardly seemed to express the depths of his heart, and his gaze was not as frank and sympathetic as it had been at other times.

At first I thought it was melancholy, that sickness which from time to time imposes somber thoughts on all men and obliges them to see darkness in everything, even in a sky resplendent with sunlight . . . . Yes, at first I thought it must be the blues which draped my young visitor in such a foul mood.

"You haven't seen me these last two months. It's because I've been on vacation in Ndimi, my native village. I came back yesterday. School will begin tomorrow . . . ."

"And your parents, how are they?"

"Very well. Except that my mother was pricked by a thorn in her garden one day. I took her to a clinic, and when I left, she was in perfect health."

Explaining all that to me in an expressionless tone of voice, he maintained an unrelentingly somber appearance.

"One might say, my friend, that you are hiding something behind this gloomy countenance. Ah, I understand why you're looking like an old man who has just lost his life's companion! You're undoubtedly brooding about all those worries awaiting you on the threshold of the new school year."

I said it jokingly. I believed that was the way to draw him out of his apparent sadness. His only response was an ironic smile. A long silence fell between us. Our eyes followed the dramas which passersby gratuitously offered us. Evening was falling. The bustle occasioned by people leaving factories, workshops, and offices had died with the setting sun. Then everything was calm. . . .

"Alas! he sighed suddenly. "Why hide it from you, my friend, I've been fired."

"What?" I cried out with a start.

"It was me, you know, who taught the first classes in that school two years ago. The day before yesterday, when I went to the administrative office, the decision to dispense with my services was communicated to me. . . . If it had been at the beginning of the vacation, I would not have given myself the trouble of coming back. In the village, I could have helped my parents with their tasks. I requested prior notice and the reimbursement of my transportation costs . . . . But . . . ."

His voice became tearful and began to tremble. A great sorrow obstructed his throat. In the twilight shadow, I perceived two pearls gleam and run down his beardless cheeks. Without asking him the reasons for his unexpected disgrace, I contented myself with becoming inwardly angry: "Oh, how wicked men are! Even those who make a profession of preaching human charity . . . ! Why torture a poor young citizen who . . . . .
I myself would have cried too, I think, if I had continued to pose such disturbing questions. I remained silent, and I listened.

"And I who thought the grounds were of a strictly professional nature, and more serious in a different way . . . !"

My indignant words comforted my young friend. And it was in an off-hand tone of voice that he continued: "If it hadn't been for that woman, a seamstress . . . ! Do they realize that I couldn't do otherwise, if I wanted to survive? How much did they pay me? A miserable salary of one thousand five hundred francs. What can one do with such a salary, especially here in Yaounde where everything must be bought . . . ? If it hadn't been for her, I would have starved to death; I wouldn't even have had a place to stay, or the force to do my work. And what work. . . ? To remain standing all day long, to shout one's self hoarse in front of restless, chattering, undisciplined, whining little brats who are constantly breaking your eardrums. A dog's life!"

He suddenly interrupted himself. He took out a handkerchief. He wiped his eyes and his forehead for a long time. He noisily blew his nose, and then, getting up, he growled in a choking voice, "the villains!"

*
*   *

He was a young man about nineteen years old. He had an athletic gait, and his expression — always smiling, always affable — seemed to defy his uncertain future.

Armed only with a school-leaving certificate, enthusiasm and a willingness to carry his humble stone for the construction of his country, he had seen himself appointed headmaster of a small school. And he had consecrated himself body and soul to the accomplishment of his task, paying no heed to his paltry salary. A true apostleship.

I will always remember the visit I paid one day to his "medieval" school. Classes were held in an old chapel and contained more than a hundred scribblers in a single room. With one arm amputated as a result of having been badly shaken by stormy weather, the large cross which dominated the nave had begun to lean, and it threatened to fall down. Its raffia-mat roof, amply nibbled by insatiable nations of termites, threatened to fall down. Its mud walls, scarred with crevices which yawned in places like large windows, threatened to fall down and take their emaciated poles with them. . . .

The pupils, completely white with dust, were like little phantoms seated on wooden logs. To read or write, they placed the spelling books or slates on their laps.

51

When they saw me approach, they stood up and welcomed me with a powerful "Good morning, sir!"

The teacher motioned me to his chair in front of a rickety set of wooden shelves which served him as a desk. He showed me his class rosters. And while I was admiring his beautiful handwriting, he explained to me that each year his best pupils were sent to continue their studies in another school where all the different classes were taught in separate rooms.

To tell the truth, whenever the master's eye turned away from the children for even the shortest interval, they transformed the classroom into a witches' sabbath. From the corner of my eye, I witnessed an animated scene running its course in front of us. Some of the pupils got up with a display of grinning gestures. They danced frenetically and then froze for a moment to beat time. They looked at us, holding their eyes wide open with their fingers and thumbing their noses. They stuck out their tongues, then fluttered their lips together, making strange burbling sounds. . . . Others got up and sat down successively in an irregular motion. At one point, they lay down on top of each other. At another, they crawled along the floor to tease a group of comrades seated elsewhere. They vociferated, beating a neighbor who seemed to be taking the lesson seriously . . . . In one part of the room, a young fellow armed with a razor blade was practicing incisions on the forearm of a young comrade. In another, someone else was thrusting a pin into a little girl's ear . . . . The most unruly of all was certainly a large boy about eight years old. He played one prank after another; he poured dust over the heads of his fellow pupils, while proclaiming in a loud voice: "I baptize you in the name of the Father, of the Son, and of the Holy Ghost, Amen!" Clouds of dust were floating everywhere, books and slates were flying about, and blows were being exchanged in a hubbub resembling that of a village marketplace. The weakest ones cried in response to insults and humiliations before running to us to complain. . . .

The master always punished the accused. He either applied blows of the ruler to the palms of their hands, or he had them kneel down with their arms extended horizontally. Suddenly, I saw him grab an iron bar. I shuddered, believing at first that it was intended for the more recalcitrant pupils. I was still shuddering when he gave a solid blow to an automobile rim hanging in the corner; it was the school bell. Silence reestablished, the class again began to run its course.

"Who knows how to recite 'The Cat and the Mice'?"

There was an enormous rush of raised hands accompanied by a salvo of young voices crying out and vying with each other: "I do, sir! I do, sir!" A little girl was chosen, and with her meowing voice, she intoned her recitation. She did it with such an expressive mimicry that no one could have avoided laughing and applauding . . . .

"What is the name of the letter written on the blackboard?"

A renewed rush of raised hands accompanied by a renewed salvo of young voices shouting, "I know, sir," was heard. The designated pupil quickly got up and replied at the top of his voice, "The letter written on the blackboard is called teeee. . . ."

"Very good," congratulated the master.

I turned toward the place upon which all eyes were still fixed. To my great surprise

I noticed that the blackboard wasn't black at all. It was a simple unpainted square of wood attached to the wall. I smiled to myself and reflected. "Having seen a blackboard in every classroom he ever attended, this young teacher undoubtedly believes that all boards are black."

I was still smiling, when frightened shouts were suddenly heard. The children got up as a single body. With stupefaction in their eyes, they scattered in all directions. They made a movement toward us, crying out, "a snake, a snake!" The master immediately armed himself with a stick and leaped to the aid of his flock. He killed the snake, but not a single child still possessed the courage to install himself in the sinister corner.

"It's like that almost every day," the master explained to me.

I got up to leave. As in a ritual, the whole class also got up and vigorously chorused a "Good-bye, sir" that will echo in my ears for the rest of my life.

How happy he was, this young teacher, my friend! How happy he was in the classroom, which housed snakes and threatened to collapse from one moment to the next. How happy he was in his classroom with wooden shelves which served as a desk, with a blackboard which wasn't black at all, with restless, chattering little brats who resembled palm birds, with his paltry salary of one thousand five hundred francs. . . ! But why did they take his happiness away from him? There is no act more cruel than depriving a human being of that which he considers to be his happiness.

I thought of all the weak persons who are crushed in this world by the wickedness of the powerful, and my heart contracted with indignation. I thought of all the efforts put forth by my young friend to instruct his little brothers. The villains! They dared fire him, abandon him, without a single franc of charity. Communion, mass, a woman of ill repute . . . ! What does all that have to do with it, when it's a question of fighting against illiteracy in our young country? The villains! Yes, men are wicked! Even those who make a profession of preaching charity according to Jesus Christ . . . ! But Jesus Christ recommends forgiving one's neighbor, at least seventy-seven times seven times. They dare make a profession of preaching human charity! The villains. . . !

The first day of school did not go without a fuss. Finding themselves confronted by a new teacher, all the inhabitants of the neighborhood expressed their indignant disapproval to him. A few fanatics threatened him vociferously. Several private meetings were organized, and a motion was enacted, demanding the reinstatement of the disgraced teacher.

Would it be possible to have more eloquent proof of the respect and confidence he enjoyed among the pupils' parents? I doubt it. The little urchins themselves didn't remain silent. Nearly all of them had the crestfallen air of orphans who had recently been subject to some cruel bereavement. And nearly all of them lodged an appeal for "their own teacher." Now, the young schoolmaster lived in the neighborhood, and he could see them from his house. They even followed him to my hut. And it was a time for one of them to show his notebook or another to recite "The Cat and the Mice" in an emotion-filled voice. In this manner we passed several long and charming moments with these naive souls.

These apparently harmless and insignificant details cause an extremely delicate aspect of the extremely serious school problem to loom up in the conscience of anyone who reflects a little bit. As soon as anything out of the ordinary hinders the smooth running of the educational system, the pupil's parents inevitably feel themselves injured in their own most hallowed interests. Nobody can deny it. School teachers and headmasters of educational institutions thus find themselves confronted by a category of persons whose tastes are often difficult to satisfy. Nevertheless, only a climate of love and discipline can make the school into a true family within human society.

It is generally admitted that the parents of school children have the right to choose the color of the education to be given their sons and daughters. But does one also have to accord them the right to choose the teacher of their preference? It is really to you, reader, that the question is being posed.

IX

KAZABALAKA

When I hear shouts echoing through the neighborhood and realize that the entire population is running toward one particular place, I know infallibly that an event is taking place.

On that afternoon, waves of people were rolling toward the Chief's compound in Nlong Kak. What was all the agitation about?

A young urchin struggled futilely in the grasp of an old woman, who was shouting at the top of her lungs, invoking her deceased parents, her deceased grandparents, and all the other dead souls in her genealogical tree. . . !

She continued to shout at the top of her lungs, as a steadily growing crowd encircled her and showered her with increduous glances.

"What is it, Edzimbi . . . ? And what has the child done to make you so excited?"

The old woman didn't reply to the Chief's question, but she did continue her endless lament while shedding an occasional tear.

"Edzimbi, tell me Edzimbi . . . !" he shouted at her again, this time with a certain uneasiness in his voice.

She remained silent for an instant; then, readjusting the worn-out rags she was wearing, she approached the Chief. Suddenly, the boy succeeded in liberating himself from her feeble grip and tried to run off until a young bystander caught hold of him. The child began to emit a series of heart-rending wails.

"Good . . . !" bellowed Edzimbi as she approached the boy's captor. "Hold him tightly, Bomba my grandson, and all my blessings shall be yours! Hold him tightly. This little rogue has just heaped shame and humiliation on me!"

At these words, scandalized cries were heard.

"Akogo, you heard how he insulted me, didn't you?" she called a young girl standing behind her to serve as a witness.

Akogo nodded her head.

The little boy had insulted the venerable Edzimbi, and, mortally wounded in her grandmotherly self-esteem, she was lodging her complaint with the Chief of Nlong-Kak.

"Very well!" he exclaimed and immediately sent for the delinquent boy's mother.

Several minutes later, after she had arrived, the trial proceeded without interruption.

"Bella, see how you educate your children . . . ! See how Olama has just publicly insulted Edzimbi!" scolded the Chief.

Bella respectfully crossed her arms, cleared her throat and, with a tinge of malice in her eyes, replied, "That my son would have insulted a venerable adult like Edzimbi — :hat surprises me, Nkukuma! Especially Edzimbi . . . !"

Turning to her son, she interrogated him in a severe tome of voice. "Olama, is it true that you dared heap shame and humiliation upon Mami Edzimbi? Did you insult her? Tell me!"

The young Olama hid his face behind an old notebook which he was holding in one hand. Without saying a word he began to snivel and whimper.

See, Nkukuma. I was right a minute ago! My son has never lacked consideration for anyone! Anyone in the neighborhood can bear witness to that . . . ! How could he have allowed himself to insult Edzimbi? Especially Mami Edzimbi for whom we all have so much respect! It's not possible . . . !

These words triggered a peal of reproachful "ah's" among the bystanders.

"What. . . ? What are you saying there, Bella?" the old woman exploded with anger. "Are you trying to say that I'm the one who is lying? A thousand curses! Do you want me to take off my clothes here and now to the eternal disgrace of your son?"*

A number of people hurried to intervene, begging the old woman not to let her-self get carried away to that extent. Turning to the little Akogo, she called upon her a second time to bear witness; she clapped her hands and trumpeted, "hey-ey-ey-ey. . . ! Me myself Edzimbi Nga Mballa Ndongo!"

After imposing silence on the noisy crowd, the Chief invited Akogo to faithfully report what had happened. In a singing voice, the little girl gave an account of the entire episode. . . .

As she and her grandmother Edzimbi were passing along the street near the small neighborhood market, they encountered Olama returning from school with his two companions Metila and Ada. They were holding hands in such a way that they blocked the entire street. Edzimbi scolded them and demanded that they break their chain. Metila and Ada obeyed without saying a word, but Olama insolently cried out, "Casablanca!"

After little Akogo's deposition, the Chief interrogated Olama, but Olama was still snivelling. "Ah, Nkukuma! Do you mean to say you don't believe little Akogo! A thousand curses . . . !" shouted Edzimbi. "My granddaughter and I have always been appalled by lying! And today everyone is actually taking us for liars . . . ! Hey-ey-ey-ey! Me myself Edzimbi Nga Mballa Ndongo. . . !"

"Hei-kyei kei-lei kei-lei ei-ei!" cried the Chief. "Who among the people here is already taking you and your granddaughter for liars?"

---

*Among the Beti in Cameroon, an older person sometimes undresses in front of a child or young man in order to lay a curse upon him.

"Everybody! And they're laughing at me as if I were a scatterbrained idiot. To insult me! Me, *Kazabalaka* . . . !"

Redoubled bursts of laughter echoed through the excited crowd.

"Ah, for the good old days!" recommenced the old woman, complaining, visibly angered. "These days no one knows where human society is going any more! And all because of those ghostlike men who come from beyond the seas and allow themselves to teach their insolent 'sab-sabi-yes' to even the smallest of our snotty-nosed brats! That's why I'm being called *Kazabalaka* today. . . !"

On all sides, bystanders were jostling each other and splitting their sides with laughter.

Somewhere in the tumultuous crowd, there was a young man holding a book in his hand. Gesturing with his finger, the Chief of Nlong-Kak invited him to come forward. "You who understand the white man's language, tell us without lying what the word 'Casablanca' means."

The young man didn't need to be coaxed. He explained that "Casablanca" is a Moroccan city.

Hardly had he finished speaking before old Edzimbi, more angry than ever, raised her cane menacingly and put the young man with the book to flight. She spit three times. She thundered, "Nkukuma, I see clearly that you are trying to make a fool of me! Hei-ei-ei-ei. . . ! Me myself Edzimbi Nga Mballa Ndongo! You dare consult one of those embryonic fellows who doesn't yet have the slightest notion about the language of the ghostlike men! According to an old woman's memory, *Kazabalaka* is a malicious insult!"

At these words, the crowd became increasingly mirthful. One could see men and women holding their sides from having laughed so heartily. In the midst of this general hullabaloo and while the elderly plaintiff was cursing, spitting with anger, threatening to take off her clothes here and now, invoking her deceased parents, her deceased grandparents, and all the other dead souls in her genealogical tree, the Chief condemned Olama's mother Bella to pay the sum of one thousand francs to Edzimbi Nga Mballa Ndongo!

Immediately mollified, the old woman pushed her grandaughter Akogo in front of her and disappeared, hobbling along and leaning on her cane.

"To call me *Kazabalaka!*" she repeated endlessly. "Me *Kaza*, and at the same time *Balaka* . . . ! God is there to judge!"

CATS' TAILS TALES

CATS' TAILS TALES
(Scenes of Cameroonian Life)

*To my beloved elder brother Dr. Hubert Nkoulou, who became
adept in the whiteman's sciences in order not to forget those which
govern this Black Africa of ours.*

Preface

If a story is enthralling, even when it remains hard to believe, the white man, eyes popping out of his head, never fails to exclaim "What a cock-and-bull story!" As for the black man, and more particularly for the Beti of Cameroon, he will burst out laughing and tell you "minlan mi nkonn essinga:" that is to say, literally: "What a tale of a cat's tail!"

That is how the somewhat unusual, not to say curious, title adorning this collection of short stories might be explained to the non-initiate.

To compose them, I listened to what was being said and looked at what was being done around me. These are therefore tales which water their roots in authentic scenes of African life. But who could blame me for having indulged my romantic fantasies, for having stretched a few episodes until they became tainted with improbability? No one but a philistine would ever broach the subject.

For their enlightenment, I would merely say that the writer is not a photographer, even in the broad sense of the word. And yet, what photographer would claim that he could reproduce an object on paper exactly as it appears to the naked eye?

The writer's role, it is true, consists of scrutinizing nature closely in order to invent beings and situations not provided by nature. Otherwise, there would never be a single truly original work of literature. Yet, it is through originality that the writer's creative power expresses itself.

There are very few Africans who will fail to see themselves profiled here and there, indicted in one fashion or another, on the following pages. In advance, I disclaim responsibility for any litigation which might result from completely accidental resemblences between names or traits attributed to my characters and those of real persons living or dead.

It is possible that, through lack of sufficient talent, I have not succeeded, as I had sincerely hoped, in helping the reader pass a few pleasurable moments in the company of these five CATS' TAILS TALES. However, one thing is certain; I will at the very least deserve credit for having made my audience aware of certain practices which, like iron balls on the legs of slaves, impede the forward motion of young African nations in general and of my native Cameroon in particular.

The Author

I

BEKAMBA, RETURNED FROM THE DEAD

The little village of Mangata slept peacefully, lulled by the distant roar of the Sanaga River. A funereal silence enveloped the huts. All fires were extinguished, and not the least sign of life filtered through their walls to the outside world.

In the courtyard, which was invaded by hideous dark shades, the domestic animals seemed afraid to disturb the calm. The atmosphere was perfectly ominous. Even the dogs remained silent; these dogs, which were sometimes driven wild by the slightest swaying of tree branches in the passage of a harmless breeze, now barely managed a few feeble yelps and, faithful sentries that they were, kept one ear to the wind as they fell asleep once more on the thresholds of the huts.

Suddenly, every animal's head, every muzzle and every snout, was seemingly beset by the same fit of nervousness. Sheep and pigs stampeded noisily in all directions. Drawing themselves nimbly erect on the tips of their paws and turning toward one of the huts, the dogs ripped apart the little village's repose with a vigorous chorus of "gbo-gbo-gbo. . . ."

Impossible to keep one's eyes closed during that salvo of barks. There was no end to it, for it was being fueled by a highly unusual sound. Someone was knocking at old Adzi Manga's door. As the raps became increasingly insistant, the fury of the dogs redoubled. But inside the house nobody stirred, and there was a reason for that.

It was in vain that the administrative authorities of Ntui preached a solidarity which ought to prevail among all citizens and, as a consequence, the hospitality due to people who traveled by night. This noctural hospitality having occasionally backfired upon the person who offered it, all the inhabitants of Mangata knew where they stood in such matters.

In particular they remembered that traveler from the Congo. After having passed the night in Ateba Awata's hut, he had implicated his host in a scandalous gold-smuggling operation. The innocent Ateba came out of the affair with three unjustifiable months in prison, and since then, all the inhabitants of Mangata knew where they stood in such matters. If some unknown person came knocking at their door late at night, they had already sworn to remain more mute than tombstones.

Nevertheless, the blows of a fist continued to shake the ludicrous bark door, and a voice continued to repeat obstinately, "It's me, Bekamba; it's me in person! Let me in! Even you, oh father, do you not recognize my voice? Poor me!"

All ears are wide open. They try to identify the inflections of that voice alternatingly hoarse, screeching, muted, and gasping for breath. It seems unlike the voice of any person living that night in Mangata. Rather, one might call it the voice of an invalid who, after a long coma, had just recovered the use of speech.

Crimson with horror, Adzi Manga at first believes that he is living in the thick fog of bad dream. Now and then he holds his breath; though inaudible, the sound of it frightens him. The throbbings of his heart also frighten him; to his ears, they are the tactless boomings of a bamboo drum. His own cane bed sometimes becomes so talkative at the least movement. Teeth clenched, he strains to make it comply with the law of silence and inertia.

Misfortune never visits all men on the same day. A turn for everyone. Yesterday it was Ateba Awata and many others. Today he is the chosen one . . . .Adzi Manga, harrassed by a sense of doom, can't prevent himself from shivering. he knows that some spirits are reincarnated at night to come and haunt the living. The best course to follow is never answering back. Thus, he continues to hold his lips hermetically sealed together. In his mind, anyone calling him "father, oh father" can only be an evil spirit, or perhaps a practical joker from one of the occult societies . . . . A thousand tombs! To call upon him like that, when the entire neighborhood knows where his only son is hanging out these days . . . ? Besides, what other Bekamba could it be, he inwardly asks himself, remembering that there were at least a dozen Bekambas in the tribe. Perhaps one of them is bringing him some important message . . . !

As a matter of fact, there are his cousins Bekamba Edongo, Bekamba Nyimi and Bekamba Atangana. There are his nephews Bekamba Ombedé and Bekamba Manga. There are the nephews of his cousin Ovoundi—Bekamba Alima and Bekamba Abouna. There is also Bekamba Koungou, an elderly maternal uncle whose rheumatism had condemned him for life to the fireside. Finally there is Bekamba Okali, the grandson of one of his brothers. However, he is working in Nkongsamba. Even supposing that he has received a leave of absence, he would have sent a letter announcing his arrival. And then, there being no paddler on the Nachtigal ferry at that hour, who in the world could have transported Bekamba Okali across the great river. . . ?

After this cursory census, no one remains in his village elder's memory, except the ominous image of one other Bekamba—of one only, and the memory of him inflicts the old man with a sudden surge of pain.

*

*   *

They had been two cousins of the same age. Having gone on a fishing expedition, they had not returned to the village by the next day.

Had they dared spend the night on one of the numerous small islands which dot the extremely rugged bed of the Sanaga River? That was hardly believable. In this month of September, the rising floodwaters swell to a relentless and devastating fury. Even the greatest fisherman take pains to avoid venturing upon them at night.

The men had departed early in the morning to look for them. When they returned in the evening, their eyes were red with terror. They had hailed in all directions, but no human voice had ever responded! All that remained, half broken to pieces and lying in the craggy sinuosities of some giant rock, was a dugout canoe.

After such a report, how could anyone rule out the assumption that a drowning had occurred? Besides, two days later this assumption was destined to be confirmed by the discovery of a partially decomposed body ten kilometers downstream. After a goodly number of additional searches had remained fruitless, everyone agreed that the other corpse must have been entombed in the ravenous entrails of a cayman.

Inconsolable grief at Mangata. The funeral celebration lasted for one moon. All day and all night long, the *essani** drums contribute their disconcerting notes to this atmosphere of two-fold mourning. The unprecedented calamity doesn't leave the elders and the village wise men indifferent, and in order to limit its effects, they organize the appropriate rites. People weep a great deal for Edongo Kounou. But they weep even more for Bekamba Adzi Manga, whose body has never been found.

Then, six months later, at a time when blurred memories are beginning to restore order in the spirits of men, someone comes knocking at old Adzi Manga's door, repeating insistently: "Father, oh father, let me in. It's me, your son Bekamba, whom everyone believed to be dead. . . !"

It is unworthy for a member of the male sex to tremble forever. Furthermore, Adzi Manga is tired of trembling with every single one of his senile muscles, so he musters all his forces and gets up, saying to himself that a man can only die once. Still, he calls to his neighbors. Despite their fear, they all get up, fully decided to see with their own eyes and for the first time a man who had returned from the dead. Some of them are carrying firebrands and torches. Goggle-eyed they are as bloated with sleep as with feelings of horror. Soon, all Mangata is standing around the stranger.

The man is about forty years old. Almost naked, he is wearing no more than a few scraps of fish net tied around his hips as a sort of loin cloth. On the ground in front of him is lying a large basket which exudes an odor of smoked fish. Whenever a villager raises his light in an attempt to recognize the man, the latter calls him by name. "Hey! Is it true that you don't recognize me either, you too . . . !"

My word, how can one so easily recognize a relative believed dead for six whole moons and for whom the entire region had attended funeral celebrations? A thousand tombs! Bekamba brought back to life after six whole moons, that's something which has never been seen or heard before!

The man seems very tired. Until this moment, he has been supporting himself on a long staff. Suddenly, he collapses without warning on the verandah floor just in front of the hut. After a quarter hour of contemplative silence, he declares in a voice alternately hoarse, screeching, muted, and gasping for breath:

"It's me Bekamba Adzi Manga in person. I was dead, drowned at the same time

---

*A war dance in honor of an illustrious dead man

65

as my brother Edongo Kounou. Do I have to say it to you again? All the noise from our funerals, we heard it every day and every night in the land of the phantoms. When we arrived, we were confined to the bottom of a gloomy cave. Each day, a woman fed us the same way a mother bird feeds her little ones. Our stomachs were not large enough to store all the dishes she placed before us, dishes invariably composed of fresh fish and marinated cassava. It's the only dish which phantoms eat. What a happy people!

"After nine days and nine nights, a phantom policeman came to open the enormous stone gates of our mysterious prison. To tell you truthfully, my eyes have never seen and will never again in my lifetime see so many people, neither in Yaounde, nor in Douala, nor anywhere else. And what people! Whole anthills of creatures all uniformly white from head to foot, with eyes absolutely white like the full moon . . . . In that place, there are neither blacks nor reds, nor albinos, nor half-breeds. Nothing but whites, and they are whiter than any white man you have ever seen. . . . Hut after hut as far as the eye can reach—large white huts like mountains of flour. And armies of white monkeys frolicking in the white dust of the courtyards, with nothing to fear from the white buffaloes, elephants, caymans, panthers and lions standing about.

"In that place, every day is a holiday, but also a working day. All of them who are capable of doing so work to feed that immense community, in which the laws of true fraternity reign harmoniously. And the work is organized in such a way that no one ever feels tired. Without interruption, soft music envelopes you in a sweet voluptuousness; and it all emanates from *mvets, balafons,* tamborines and *algaitas** which are scarcely ever seen . . . !

"They brought us before a great assembly of old men whose heads were as bald as calabashes. The one who was presiding asked our names. He asked our names and the names of our fathers and the names of our grandfathers. We had barely finished conjugating our genealogical trees, when an old fellow suddenly rose from his corner and shouted an oath of war. It was our grandfather in person, Manga Kounou whom we had the opportunity of meeting for the first time. He died, as you know, only a few days after we were born. The venerable ancestor came and embraced us. He was proud and happy to see once again the young offshoots from the blood of his blood. However, having turned his back upon us, he began to fulminate against all those who were present. He couldn't understand why phantom-policemen had arrested us — my brother Edongo Kounou and myself—during a peaceful fishing expedition. It wasn't yet time for us to abandon the sun of the living. He thundered, mad with rage, contending that the other phantoms were joyously plotting the extermination of his line. In conclusion, he insisted that these unjustified arrests of his descendants cease immediately.

"Then a great palaver broke out. 'The waters of the Sanaga,' retorted several speakers, 'swallow the fisherman of Mangata just as easily as those from other villages, for all of them are flouting the laws of the great river's Goddess-Mother. Disobedient,

---

*An mvet is a stringed instrument played by traditional story-tellers and singers. A balafon is a wooden xylophone with gourd resonators, and an algaita is a wooden clarinette characteristic of North Cameroon.

they continue to fish the bay of Okundi, precisely the spot where her venerable residence is located. Selfish, they hardly trouble themselves to pay the tax which she demands of them and which by rights is levied against the first catch of the year . . . .'

"A few voices support our worthy ancestor's complaints and protestations, and they succeed in procuring our return to natural life.

"However, the day before yesterday, before the way back can be opened to us, they discover, alas, that my brother Edongo Kounou's hour of death has just tolled. You can imagine my consternation. I can't restrain my tears. But the sound of my heart-rending sobs merely irritates the people of the phantom realm. It's apparent to them that he is being spared what men call suffering! While you here were bewailing our tragic loss, he on the other hand was mortally offended. He can't understand why the living mourn the dead so much, for it seems to him that the former are less happy than the latter. Yes. . . seeing me cry, all the phantoms, including Manga Kounou, became exceedingly angry. Then, after having burdened me with this basket of dried fish as a sort of viaticum, their policemen pursue me with a vigorous lashing of whips to the bank of the great river.

"That is why, fathers and mothers, brothers and sisters, I have come back alone today, alone and without my brother Edongo. Alone, but the bearer of important messages and the possessor of enormous powers. With all my heart, I hope that the inhabitants of Mangata shall be the first to benefit from them. Doesn't a well-known proverb say, and rightly so, that any bearer of good news belongs above all to his family? But all the worse for you, if you want none of it. Already, you are refusing to recognize me, me Bekamba Adzi Manga. . . ! How many times did I knock at the door before anyone deigned to respond or let me in? It's true that I was dead; oh, poor me! But all the worse for you, I say . . . ."

The tone of Bekamba's voice becomes alternatingly mournful and threatening. From the group of villagers gathered around him at a respectable distance and listening with eyes and ears wide open, a few tentative, apprehensive exclamations emerge, "Ay-kyay, ay-kyay! Why this harsh tone for your own people?"

No, it hadn't been easy to recognize Bekamba Adzi, the only son of Adzi Manga. His frightfully dazed eyes were popping from his head, and they were incapable of focusing on a single person for any length of time. His gestures were awkward, like those of someone under the spell of a *kong*.* His skin looked so hard and leathery that it seemed to have been scourged continuously for six moons. Yes, he had become nearly unrecognizable. But here and there, a few indelible marks and identifying characteristics allowed all his close friends and relatives to make out what he had previously been.

Little by little, doubt vanished. That reddish skin of false albinos, those hammer-like toes so well endowed with nails, that generously turned-up nose and that face strewn with freckles left little room for uncertainty. Each member of the tribe conducted his own examination, drawing one step nearer, stretching his neck, and staring fixedly. And if a well-known swelling or scar was discovered, someone would point to it from

---

*a type of witchcraft in which spells are cast by incantation

a distance and affirm loudly, "It's him all right, Bekamba Adzi, the only son of Adzi Manga!"

It is necessary to tell you that in our little backwater settlements the craziest stories circulate freely and always encounter people willing to accept them at face value. Thus, there was nothing astonishing about the inhabitants of Mangata lending a credulous ear to this fantastic account about a land of phantoms. Indeed, everyone had but a single fear. It was that a phantom, attracted by the still fresh scent from their part of the country, might return to perpetrate a second abduction on the person of Bekamba Adzi Manga.

The elders and the village wise men took counsel and reached agreement. That very night, Bekamba Adzi was riddled with incisions and bathed in exorcisms. Following that, there were magnificent festivities. In every heart, they effaced half the wounds left by the funeral celebrations of six months ago.

*
*   *

Bekamba did not wait long to communicate his important messages and to exercise his immense powers.

Each day, his old father's little hut was filled to the breaking point. All the villagers came to request news about some deceased relative or to ask for advice about some personal problem. And Bekamba, who had returned from the dead, stated with the most solemn tone in the world that he had seen—seen with his very own eyes—all the dead members of the tribe, back to the father of the father of his grandfather.

"You too, I saw your father; he is not satisfied with the way in which you have treated his wives. Why chase them away when they should be perpetuating his presence and his memory? And you too, your twin brother forbids you from now on to participate in the hunting of caymans; you run the risk of killing him in that form some-day. . . ! And you there, your mother advises you to return to the first husband your father chose for you. Otherwise, there is no hope that you will ever become a mother some day . . . ! And you over there, your daughter entrusted me with a remedy for you; your illness is no longer incurable."

Consulted, listened to, and believed, as all "righters of wrongs" usually are, Bekamba saw himself constantly surrounded by his people, and, in time, crowned with a halo of unparalleled popularity. It did not take long for his reputation to spread far, very far from Mangata. The inhabitants of neighboring villages and those from distant villages; those from the other side of the Mbam River and those from the other side of the Sanaga, all came running feverishly as if they were hurrying toward the cradle of a new-born Messiah. And they returned satisfied, for they all received something: this one a timely warning, that one a medical prescription, and that other one a protective *gris-gris** . . . .

Soon, a problem arose. It was necessary to provide shelter for the crowds which

---

*an amulet or charm thought capable of warding off evil

thronged endlessly to Mangata. At first, rudimentary sheds were hastily erected at random all over the village courtyard. Afterwards, several days were spent constructing a large hut for the more seriously ill patients and for those who had come from afar.

At the very beginning, Bekamba was generous in his own way; he exacted nothing from his clients, except the duty of listening to him and scrupulously following his instructions. Two weeks later, he requested a payment of five francs, at first timidly and then quite openly. Finally, encouraged by a few successes, he no longer hesitated to collect more substantial honoraria.

A few successes? To be sure . . . ! Yes, there were successes, because horrible demons did depart from people's stomachs; because nagging rheumatisms were silenced in people's joints; because, finally, in the presence of the good man of Mangata, the man who had returned alive from the land of the dead, all good souls felt as if they themselves had been born again beneath the sun of the living . . . !

For him, incurable illnesses didn't exist, even among the patient multitudes of blind men and cripples! However, the operations he prescribed to get them back into shape proved so complicated that they could never have been performed. It would have been necessary, for example, to obtain "excrement from a lightning bolt," musk from a civet cat, leopard brains, crocodile fat, chimpanzee bones. . . .

A vast flood of people continued to flow toward Mangata. Step by step the little village discarded its gloomy rustic attire and began to dress up, from morning to evening, in all the finery of a country fair or a shrine for pilgrims — a fair where all prices were licit, a shrine where all sects were allowed.

Moslems in their flowing gandourahs could be seen there. Seated upon hallowed sheepskins and with their eyes toward Mecca, they murmured verses from the Koran in mysterious tones, while piously banging their heads against the ground . . . .

Protestants could be seen there. Armed with copies of the Bible and casting their eyes mysteriously toward the infinite, they now and then bawled out hymns at the top of their lungs.

Catholics could be seen there in great numbers, invading every corner of the place. Their eyes devoutly focused upon a little statue installed in a temporary shed, they intoned endless rosaries, which were occasionally interrupted by solemn chants. They invoked Mary, they praised Mary, they implored Mary . . . ! Not any old Mary! But "Mary the holy virgin, Mother of Jesus" or "Mary the holy virgin, daughter of the Jews" or "Mary the holy virgin, wife of Joseph, the old carpenter from Nazareth . . . ."

To tell the truth, the cacophony which arose from that Babel of voices was exemplary. And no one, faced with this hodgepodge of believers in such diverse religions, would have had any idea what it was all about. For all of them were expecting temporal salvation from a man who was neither marabout, nor pastor, nor priest, but who claimed to have spent six moons in the land of phantoms. And submerged beneath this devoted and obedient human sea, Bekamba had become important, invisible, illustrious . . . like all great persons in this world.

After five months of this ludicrous business, he had not only enriched himself, but even more than that, he was reputed to have become the wealthiest peasant in the whole district. His herd of sheep and his flock of chickens multiplied before one's very eyes. Every day, his pockets were fattened with sizeable sums of money.

And what about women? Ah well, Bekamba, returned from the dead, had only too many to choose from.

Is it necessary to tell you that in this world women are the creatures most concerned about their own happiness? Go to any health center, and you will meet women, countless women overrunning the place! Make your way into any "House of God," and you will find women, countless women overrunning the place! Venture, finally, to take a few steps beneath a sorcerer's roof, and you will undoubtedly come across women, countless women overrunning the place . . .! And then, tell me, what woman—even if she is endowed with the best health in the world—does not lovingly cultivate her own "little infirmity?" There are none. And such a woman would move heaven and earth to get rid of it, to remain a virgin in all matters of physical or spiritual illness. It's because in this world women are the creatures most concerned with their own happiness . . . !

Thus, blindly confident, women and more women came to Mangata in hopes of achieving happiness. They came in small groups and in long columns. They came from neighboring villages and from distant villages, from villages on the other side of the Mbam and from villages on the other side of the Sanaga. Their eyes were wide-open, filled with tears and anguish.

But each of them was intent upon receiving the best treatment. In any case, they did not fail to stage tragi-comic scenes for everyone to see. The most apprehensive, the most impatient, and the most nervous lost no time in showing what kind of wood their fires were stoked with. They didn't shrink from profaning the public prayers, and everywhere people were shouting "scandal," and people where shouting "sacrilege."

Sometimes they could be heard literally showering each other with curses and insults. Sometimes they could be seen jostling their way through the crowd, exchanging punches, preparing to trip somebody or themselves biting the dust, or proudly tearing each other's dresses and underpants to shreds. They not only argued over Bekamba's medicine, but also over his little smiles, his eloquent glances and also . . . oh-la-la . . . his recently purchased enormous metal bed. The primary concern, which, it appears, motivated all of them, was to put an end to that peaceful illness which most frequently gives all black women insomnia—sterility.

The whole affair acquired a certain notoriety, and the entire region was being disturbed by it. Impossible not to attract the vigilant attention of the administrative authorities. They are there to make certain that public order is maintained. They are there to protect the weaker from the stronger, but also to protect the greatest fools from the shrewdest villains in the land. That is why, one fine morning, Bekamba, followed at increasingly respectable intervals by his numerous admirers, entered the premises of the police station at Ntui. He was the bearer, no longer of important messages, but of a small, a very small summons.

*

*   *

His arrival was greeted with shakings of heads, curious glances, pointing fingers and voices whispering, respectfully whispering, "There he is, the man from Mangata who returned from the dead."

All that puffed up Bekamba with pride, with the sort of pride which bestows upon one's head the right to sit firmly in place above one's two shoulders.

What? Pride in a police station . . . ? Well, yes, and why not, especially when one bears the sacred title, "he who has returned from the dead?" Just think . . . ! With all the commotion his name had aroused, with all the prestige he enjoyed, Bekamba knew that he would not have been invited to this place, which usually inspires shudders of fear, unless someone had wanted him to perform one of those prodigious feats that had made him the man of the hour.

"Certainly," he said to himself, "the honorable chief of police must be in a terrible fix. These functionaries! Each of them has his own private little cancer. For them, I will double my fees; they have money to burn."

Bekamba was introduced into a spacious room where a vapor of brutal majesty seemed to be floating in the air. In every corner the personal effects of vanquished criminals were sleeping— arrows, cutlasses, matchetes, clubs, spears, hunting rifles— and all of them were being carefully guarded by little hand-printed cardboard labels.

The chief of police was installed behind a desk filled with file-folders and notebooks. Since he had not seen anyone enter, he didn't move. With the same attentive guesture, he continued to initial the various papers spread out in front of him. Suddenly, after having rapidly shuffled the file-folders back into order, he raised his head and countered Bekamba's mischievous stare with a severe, imposing stare of his own. Then, with a careless wave of the hand, he designated a chair for him.

In sitting down, Bekamba smiles to himself. The merciful and protective smile of those who know that they are in the possession of immense powers. He listens to his heart galloping impatiently like a horse headed toward the Land of Cockaigne.

All of a sudden, the door opens and several functionaries enter, their expressions alternatingly distrustful, astonished, and full of anger. The chief asks a question. In reply, Bekamba speaks in a steady voice, with all the assurance of an infallible magus. All ears are listening to him, and not a single mouth gives the lie to what he is saying. And because he is convinced that they are interested in listening to him, Bekamba pays little attention to the naive inconsistencies with which he adorns his "tale of a cat's tail." At the end of his story, there are nothing but quizzical smiles and skeptical expressions all around to greet him.

Bekamba also smiles, sanctimoniously. Until then, he had hardly troubled his head about the matter. But before long an icy shiver is gnawing at his entrails. A policeman has just burst into the room. Not a phantom-policeman, but a real policeman, a flesh-and-blood man armed with a healthy-sized riding whip! He comes to attention, adopting the attitude of a subordinate awaiting orders from his boss.

Bekamba, the man from Mangata who had returned from the dead, understands nothing any more. Nothing at all, especially when a shiver runs up his back and when the chief, having quickly gotten to his feet, orders him first to rise and then to lie down flat on his belly upon the cement floor. To say that Bekamba Adzi, son of Adzi Manga, didn't sweat blood and water that day—ah, that would be a lie. A horrifying flash of lightning shot across his eyes, which had opened wide in a perpetual questioning stare. Then he begins to realize the sort of hands he'd fallen into.

Oh, miserable quarter hours are not to the taste of every mouth. Try to imagine how that of Bekamba Adzi is transformed—Bekamba Adzi, son of Adzi Manga, the prestigious man from Mangata who had returned from the dead. His face came to life with tics, grimaces, and wrinkles unworthy of a famous man. At one moment his lips stretched taut; at others, they contracted hideously, like those of a gorilla slobbering with terror.

"What is it, whatever can it be, honorable Mister Police Chief?"

"It's simply that you must tell us a little more clearly everything you saw in the land of the phantoms!" chorused the assembled functionaries, bursting with laughter.

"Flat on your stomach, and quickly!" growled the chief.

Soon, the bellowings of an animal in distress are emanating from all the doors and windows of the police station, and they are punctuated with blows of a riding whip and with enormous outbursts of laughter . . . . This spectacle lasts until our Bekamba, unable to take any more, resigns himself to begging: "Forgive me, forgive me, Honorable Mister Chief! Stop, please stop . . . ! I'm dying! Forgive me! I'll explain; I'll tell you the truth, the whole truth . . . . Allow me . . . !"

They allow Bekamba to explain himself, and Bekamba now tells a completely different story, the true one.

*
*   *

Edongo Kounou and Bekamba Adzi had frequently had their little disagreements, particularly in regard to a countrywoman who offered herself to both of them. Ah yes, some women like that sort of thing: setting two brothers, two friends, at loggerheads in order to laugh at both of them for the rest of their lives.

Worried about the little community's tranquillity, the elders called several counsels. Such scandalous dissension had no place among two branches of the same tribal tree. Following the appropriate procedure for this kind of conflict, the two cousins were made to drink publicly from the same cup of palm-wine, while swearing an oath to forget everything. . . . They swore to forget everything and especially the charms of that woman of ill fortune.

Now, it became necessary to prove that they had been reconciled. It became necessary to prove it by strolling about together as they had previously done, and, also as they had previously done, by going out together to pursue their customary occupations. The first time they went fishing, it appears that the weight of former quarrels again grew heavy enough to capsize their canoe.

Everywhere, the fury of the waters roared implacably. They swam, each on his own side. They swam with all the agility of their limbs. But, splash . . . ! The current carried Edongo Kounou far away.

72

After many efforts, Bekamba set foot upon a large rock. He clung to it with every single fiber in his fingers and toes. Aided by brief moments of respite, he secured a better position for himself. With all sorts of debris floating in easy reach, he constructed a makeshift platform which permitted him to climb one branch of a half-drowned tree. From there, he yelled; he yelled until evening in hope of attracting help. But no one answered him. He just barely succeeded in reaching one of the tree's upper branches. It was there that he passed the night—a sleepless and frozen night, filled with the buzzing of mosquitoes. . . .

Early the next morning, still shivering with cold, he returned to do battle against the impetuous waves. A good swimmer, he dove off in the direction of a little lost island which never completely disappears, even during the season when the year's floodwaters reach their peak. He had frequently gone there with other fishermen. After two hours of arduous swimming, he reached the "promised land."

The survivor lived there beneath an old lean-to, fishing, stuffing himself with fish, and sleeping alone in the good company of countless mosquitoes. Six months later, when the waters became calm and receded, he chose to leave this diminutive State of Savagery; he chose to leave it as the bearer of a huge basket of dried fish and also as the bearer of a story which he had fished from the turbulent waters of his own imagination.

"Yes, I was afraid, honorable Mister Chief!" Bekamba admitted, wiping aside a few remaining tears. I was very much afraid that I would be accused of having drowned my cousin Edongo Kounou, with whom I had often had rather thorny relations . . . . As a result, I was afraid of being accused in a court of law for a crime which I didn't commit."

"And all those fine things you swindle from the people?" questioned the police chief.

After emitting a thunderous laugh, Bekamba, the good man from Mangata who had returned from the dead, exclaimed, "Oh, honorable Mister Chief! As you yourself ought to know, life belongs to those who know how to take care of themselves."

II

THE PATH OF ILL-FATED LOVERS

It has certainly become trite among us here in Black Africa to say that no one dies a natural death. Indeed, even when an accident or an illness visible to the naked eye is involved, the more clairvoyant sight of a "four-eyed man" will always discover mysterious assassins at work . . . !

That's exactly what happened upon the death of old Belinga Mvondo, a respectable grower from the respectable village of Essam, hidden somewhere down there in the heart of a savannah near Nanga-Eboko.

Everyone in heaven and on earth had certainly seen Belinga Mvondo dragging his hernia after him as if it were a sack of priceless treasure. It was one of those hernias which can no longer be confined to the lower regions in a pair of pants or dissimulated in the baggy folds of an ample pagne. No! Belinga Mvondo's hernia was, people said, as old as his first wife Avouzoa. It had become a veritable social phenomenon, and he was as famous for it as he was for his wealth. Small children were afraid of it; the most intractable ones became well-behaved as soon as they were given to understand that they would be locked up in it forever and ever. As far as adults were concerned, they regarded it with astonishment and respect; they even whispered that it was in recompense for this monstrous hernia that the gods had heaped so much good fortune upon Belinga Mvondo.

Early on Avouzoa had advised him to go to the hospital at Efok or at Enongal. But Belinga Mvondo didn't want to hear anything about such matters. He objected that, before the white man arrived, it wasn't the sort of illness over which men's hearts became troubled! If one nibbled all day long on a few roots and onions and wild fruits, that would be enough to neutralize the "infirmity of noblemen!" Since men's voices always carried the force of law in traditional society, Avouzoa prudently held her tongue. She knew that married life sometimes obliges one to accept disgusting things . . . . For her, this was certainly one of them, this hernia growing peacefully between the legs of her master under God.

Moreover, as time went on, Belinga Mvondo proved that disgusting illnesses simply don't exist, except for poor people. He married a second wife, then a third one, then a fourth one, then . . . Approximately thirty years later, his concession having expanded to ten huts with adjoining kitchens, he joyously prided himself on the possession of seventeen wives, who successively supplanted each other according to the date of their arrival, their youth, and their beauty . . . .

As for beauty, one had to admit that Assomo, the last to arrive, was what could be called a young and beautiful woman. Armed with her youthful charms, she literally conquered the heart of the old hernia-sufferer. It was she who henceforth stayed in the *abaa** at the side of the common husband. It was she who filled his pipe! And again it was she who served him with food and drink . . . ! That was all very well. But where the shoe pinched most was in the fact the "rights of the marriage bed" were no longer respected. The favorite had become the chosen one in a heart which belonged equally to sixteen other women. No, things just couldn't go on like that. . . !

Because Assomo remained the only one singing and laughing with joy, Belinga Mvondo's harem was plunged into an atmosphere of mourning. The other women hardly spoke; they hardly sang; and they laughed even less. A common martyrdom gnawed away at all of them and, from that moment on, united them in a tightly-knit alliance. Naturally immurred in their own bitterness and rancor, they grumbled from one end of the day to the other. Of course they could only grumble among themselves, like a discontented but disarmed people who, with downcast eyes, resign themselves to keeping the plans for an impossible *coup d'etat* simmering in their heads. Custom was custom. It was there to choke off the first manifestation of any women's rebellion.

Before long, they were having recourse to little magical schemes intended to turn aside Belinga Mvondo's heart. Some served him dishes filled with minced cut-grass. In the middle of the night, others buried worn-out brooms in the courtyard. And finally, still others discreetly concealed whiskers and claws of wild animals beneath the common husband's bed. . . ! There were even those who contemplated a poisoning which they proposed to blame upon the innocent Assomo. Yes, a poisoning! Let no one raise the slightest doubt in this matter. Women slighted in love are capable of anything.

---

*the man's hut (as opposed to "nda," the hut of a woman)

They are still thinking about it when, one night, they hear a whining voice pierce the silence of the compound, already plunged in sleep. They wake up; they listen for a moment; then, figuring that the old fellow is probably administering some sort of punishment to his favorite, they try to get back to sleep . . . . But no. Assomo's lamentations leave no room for doubt . . . . They listen more attentively. Finally, they decide to get up, to go out . . . . Before long, as if participating in a sacred rite, they are chorusing the laments of their young fellow-wife, while saying to themselves in their hearts, "Good riddance."

Belinga Mvondo, who had always considered them as second-class wives, if not as nonentities, had abandoned them there, all of them without exception, in order to undertake a solitary journey of no return.

For whatever it was worth, they wept bitterly; they wept while rolling on the ground, hair askew and gesturing wildly . . . . Cruel deception with but a single purpose: to forestall and attenuate the malicious rumors and tortures which always accompany the rite of *akus*.* For this reason, they worked hard at crying. Crocodile tears fell from their eyes onto the motionless corpse of Belinga Mvondo. They cried and indeed acquitted themselves marvelously in regard to this duty of crying, which, following our noble customs, requires that a woman cry over her husband's corpse, bitterly and while rolling on the ground, hair askew and gesturing wildly. . . .

Once the dead man was buried, they held the solemn palaver which usually brings an illustrious person's funeral celebrations to an end.

On that day of the long dry season, the sun is shining with its most beautiful colors of fire. It fortifies the orators with uncommon zest and nervousness.

"How does it happen that Belinga Mvondo, son of Mvondo Kuma, kicks the bucket so prematurely—so prematurely, with all his teeth still in his mouth and with his head only half bald? How does it happen, eh? That's a real miracle, isn't it? Since the earth has been earth, has anyone ever seen such a thing?"

To these classic and highly embarrassing questions posed by spokesmen for the outsiders, spokesmen for the Essam tribe replied. There are explanations, clarifications and reconsiderations. They speak about Belinga Mvondo's adolescence and about his age of majority. They speak about the enterprising spirit and the courage which enabled Belinga Mvondo to climb the social ladder until he had attained a wide renown. They speak about his cocoa plantations, about his herds of animals, and about his harem, which was the pride of the entire Essam tribe. They speak about anything and everything, except that enormous hernia which for more than thirty years had grown peacefully between the legs of Belinga Mvondo.

And completely out of breath, the spokemen for the Essam conclude in sad and moving tones. "What is to be done, sons-of-our fathers, once misfortune has taken up its residence upon a people's head!"

One secret assembly succeeds another. In the end, the floor is given to a man

---

*a mourning period during which the wife or wives of a recently deceased man are obliged to undergo a series of ordeals

who attracts public attention as much by his words as by his garb, richly adorned with red feathers and glittering all over with snail shells.

"No, let's not waste our time here needlessly!" he begins with a tone of rebuke. "I have consulted my *ngam*,* and as you all know, my *ngam* is infallible! And everybody—as many of you as are here today—should realize that Belinga Mvondo, son of Mvondo Kuma, was already dead long before he actually died last night! Imagine a cornstalk surrounded by brambles and sisal-grass? Where have you seen such a thing? Tell me. And you should know that, if Belinga Mvondo hadn't been a true man of the male sex, he would have kicked the bucket long ago."

The venerable orator, for whom alone all eyes and ears had been opened wide, abruptly breaks off his speech and returns to his seat. You think he's finished with the matter? Ah, no! After having nibbled on many segments of cola nut, after having swallowed many draughts of palm wine and after having smoked many pipefuls of tobacco, he gets up once more and begins to speak again in the following terms: "Don't make us waste time, I say. Belinga Mvondo loved his youngest wife the way one loves a *gris-gris*. Belinga Mvondo loved the son-of-his-sister the way one loves a limb from one's own body. Belinga Mvondo believed himself loved by those whom he loved. . . ! What then? Why waste our time here needlessly? Ah, poor Belinga, victim of a heart overflowing with love for those nearest to him . . . !"

Eloquent murmurs run through the crowd; then there are bewildered stares, searching for Belinga Mvondo's young wife and the son-of-his-sister. It must have been them, and not the enormous hernia, which brought about the old man's "premature" death. Because the *ngam* is infallible, it could not be otherwise.

It doesn't take long for the accused to realize the fate which awaits them. They are going to be ostracized by the whole population. And what else? Alas, one never knows what traditional custom in our country can bring about, when it comes to punishing the guilty.

---

*a variety of trap-door spider employed in a type of divination also known as "ngam"

The young wife of Belinga Mvondo bursts into indignant sobs. She protests her innocence, weeping bitterly and rolling on the ground. However, no one takes her seriously. Everybody knows she is acting. As for the son of Belinga Mvondo's sister, he bursts into the courtyard. He paces back and forth, bawling out a torrent of incomprehensible words; he immediately demands the test of the *elonn*.*

"Yes, let them give me the *elonn* to drink, and quickly. The Gods will reveal whether I—Zibi Mendomo, son of Mendomo Mvondo—am the author of the premature death of my *nyandomo*** Belinga Mvondo, of the *nyandomo* who loved me so much and who was so much loved by me!"

Protests and outbursts of mocking laughter make themselves heard in every quarter. Zibi Mendomo too is not taken seriously. People see no more in him than a comedian who is also acting. The man with the *ngam* gets up again, and laughing mercilessly, he declares: "Aha. . . ! Shrewd, the little bambinos these days! Zibi Mendomo dares to demand the *elonn*, because he knows that the administrative authorities of Nanga Eboko have officially prohibited its use, which can be punished by imprisonments and fines . . . ! Graves of the dead! Little snotty-nosed brats of his sort have not been permitted to mock men and Gods with impunity as long as the earth has been earth. But it's really the white men who deserve our wrath, for they are the ones who have turned our country upside-down like this."

At these words, the crowd falls silent. The sky is heavy and the atmosphere over-heated. Nerves are mercilessly scourged by the heat, and sweat is exacted in profusion. One might almost say that the gods are preparing to drop the fiery ball on the earth's surface. But suddenly, a strange shadowy mass forms in space, and the star of day becomes little more than a shining eye and then disappears completely.

At that moment, the man with the *ngam* abruptly sits up in his lounge chair. Addressing himself to the people who have been struck dumb by the inexplicable phenomenon, he exclaims in a strong and prophetic voice: "There, you see, didn't I predict it a moment ago? A great disaster is hanging over the head of the people of Essam. Today you mourn for Belinga Mvondo; do you know, you men of no experience, how many deaths there are left for you to mourn? In the sky you can read for youselves the wrath of the gods. . . ."

And fear-filled eyes are all lifted up to read the wrath of the gods in a sky darkened by a solar eclipse.

The only way to hold this calamity in abeyance is to banish Zibi and his accomplice Assomo immediately. Immediately, I say, otherwise. . . ."

In the midst of his speech, a mob of furious young people falls upon Zibi and Assomo, dealing them powerful blows with sticks and pursuing them with volleys of stones for more than three miles outside the village of Essam.

---

*a West African tree, the extremely poisonous bark of which was used to prepare a brew that accused criminals were required to drink. If they survived the ordeal, they were presumed innocent, but if they died (as they usually did), they were presumed guilty.

**maternal uncle

*
*   *

Zibi Mendomo is plunging down a little-frequented path, hardly knowing where it might lead him. Gasping for breath, he pauses. He must find shelter, but where? Follow the highway and pass through the villages. Impossible! Everywhere the same hostility awaits him, and from every direction he sees himself being pursued. The drums of Essam never stop spreading the fatal news:

> the gods and the heavens are angered,
> a misfortune, a great misfortune is
> weighing upon the people of Essam,
> an ungrateful nephew and a faithless wife
> have caused the son of Mvondo Kuma to
> kick the bucket,
> oh what an incredible thing!
> there they are banished, banished,
> they arrive, but no hospitality
> for these two ill-fated lovers . . . . .

Zibi listens as the drums transport these venimous outcries, while the wrathful sky is becoming darker and darker. A whole nation of hideous clouds lurk among the trees' hideous tentacles. A sudden fall of night, impenetrable to the re-assuring wink of even the brightest star. Sensing calamity, the birds have prudently silenced their arduous chirping. Not even the fearless hooting of an owl. The least bush seems to hide an abyss filled with mute monsters imposing silence on all the other creatures.

Panting with emotion, Zibi holds himself erect. Confused, he asks himself what he should do. Since the day of his birth, he had never seen the sun die so quickly in the middle of the day and then give birth to a virtually miraculous night. He had grown up in the village of Essam, and he had never left it. Spoiled by his maternal uncle, he had experienced a childhood disturbed by but a single year of school. The largest grower in the large village of Essam did not for long tolerate the teacher's switch continually raking over the tender, bronze skin of his beloved nephew.

Zibi thinks about the end of the world. As a matter of fact, hadn't he heard from the mouth of a pastor that God would one day destroy the world? But nowhere had it been decreed that it would be him, Zibi Mendomo, who would bring about that end of the world! Nowhere had it been decreed that it would occur because of his love for the youngest wife of his *nyandomo,* a love which, moreover, was nothing more than that of a young man sowing his wild oats—quite permissible according to tradition! What man didn't have the right to court the wife of his *nyandomo*?

Head filled with these upsetting reflections, he for the first time feels the presence of Assomo next to him. The young widow is shaking all over with fear. Arms crossed upon her breast, she presses against him, like a lamb seeking warmth and protection beneath the belly of a ewe. And it's his turn to begin trembling. A common terror and a common anguish grip them both in a merciless embrace. In these critical moments, their love loses all its piquancy and acquires the taste of *metet*.* Zibi collapses onto the trunk of a dead tree. And so does Assomo.

For a long time, a very long time, he holds his head in his hands; his eyes are glued to the ground, which is carpeted with dark shades. He drops a plumb line into the depths of his being. For the beautiful eyes of a woman, he sees himself being precipitated into poverty. His *nyandomo*, who had never had a child of the male sex, did not conceal his last wishes. A huge cocoa plantation, herds of animals, a harem of seventeen women, an enormous prestige! To lose all that for the beautiful eyes of a woman. What misfortune! Love sometimes plays such dirty tricks on lovers!

But living every day next to a beautiful woman — who could refrain from losing his head? For that matter, couldn't one say it was Belinga Mvondo himself who had unwittingly laid the groundwork for his beloved nephew's unhappiness? That rash habit of eating every day from the same dish as his young wife and Zibi, that was not proper. Gazing at her, having his eyes filled with her, Zibi could hardly be expected to repress his amorous impulses forever. Patience, they say, has its limits. The same is true of an honest man's courage and self-possession, when he finds himself face-to-face with a beautiful woman. Oh, fate! Two expressive glances charged with mutual desire, then two broad and collusive smiles, and that is how adultery, the greatest revolution ever to shake human families, comes into being.

*

*   *

To their great satisfaction, the other wives were the first to stumble upon this clandestine love affair. At first, they whispered among themselves and let fly — oh-la-la — one of those enormous bursts of laughter which makes passersby think that a bevy of black women has just given birth to the eighth wonder of the world! Then, believing that they had found the surest means of hastening the young favorite's downfall, they perfidiously encouraged her in her unfaithfulness. Finally, taking advantage of their rare "rights of the marriage bed," they did not forget to drop a word into the husband's ear — one of those words calculated to rouse a heart which loves: "Your very own wife, the wife you adore like a God—to our great misfortune—there she is, being dragged through the mud and dust by your beloved son, behind our huts, like one of those old baskets which children drag around to amuse themselves with."

"What? Which wife? Which son?" furiously demanded Belinga Mvondo, who didn't want to believe his ears.

"How many wives do you adore, and how many sons do you love, eh?" they retorted.

Belinga Mvondo couldn't contain himself for jealously. Once, in the middle of the night, he demanded an explanation from his favorite.

What woman would be courageous enough to admit her own infidelity? There are none, and there wouldn't be one, even if she were to be surprised, still panting with excitement, beneath the voluptuous burden of a willing accomplice!

----
*a plant with very bitter leaves

Assomo was frightened. She became flustered; she scratched herself in several places. She protested energetically and profusely; she swore oaths on all the graves of her own Yemvela tribe; she heaped insults upon her fellow-wives, and she made her husband admit that jealously and jealousy alone was behind their false accusation!

After a pause, she wanted to open her mouth again and speak out, to raise her angry voice and become truly indignant at that late hour of the night. But a paternal voice intervened tenderly:

"Don't worry your little head, my beloved Assomo! I know my other wives; I know them all. Yes, they are jealous of our love! Do you think that I believed their malicious snippets of gossip for a single moment? You, the mistress of my nephew, that would have astonished me. . . !"

To allay the master's suspicions, Assomo cautioned Zibi to be on his guard. . . . From then on, the frequency of their rendezvous decreased. Far from snuffing out their love, however, the lean periods stirred it up all the more. Also, from then on, the young wife was tortured with insomnia. Next to that body smoked and dried with years, smelling of decay, and burdened with a monstrously disgusting hernia, she no longer managed to get even a wink of sleep all night long . . . ! "Why don't we run away?" she suggested one day. In matters of love, men are far from displaying the same audacity as women. "No," a trembling Zibi answered her, "it's better to await patiently the death of my old *nyandomo!*" He believed that this was the way to avoid a scandal which, alas, and despite everything, broke out in the end anyway, and in the most brutal and unexpected manner.

*

*   *

Little by little the sun re-appeared. As if by enchantment. A beautiful round, yellow sun which floods nature in its immense smile of re-assuring light. Zibi and Assomo look at each other with dazed eyes. Several minutes later, night falls heavily. True night, protectress of thieves and clandestine lovers. It spreads its cool, refreshing veil of silence and mystery over the earth.

"What do you intend to do, Assomo, now that . . . ?" mumbled the young man without looking at his companion in misfortune.

"And you?"

"Me, I'll go somewhere, anywhere! However, the annoying thing is that . . . it's that I have no alternative but to leave you behind."

"What?" burst out the young widow in a voice husky with amazement. "Leave me behind, go away from me? Have you thought long and hard before throwing that in my face? No, Zibi, one doesn't kill a dead person. Yet I am a dead person now. What have I done to you, Zibi, that you kill me a second time? Oh, how true it is that men have hearts of stone. . . !"

Lips pressed tightly together and his whole body quivering, the young man listens to these lamentations. He feels a mysterious burden weighing on his shoulders, on his head, on his heart. He had always believed in the words of sorcerers and village elders.

How can he stop believing in them now? All of them had cursed him, and he knows that henceforth a great misfortune will be hovering over his existence. It wasn't one or two inhabitants of Essam who had cursed him and driven him away, but a whole village, a whole tribe, a whole people. . . . To go away from Assomo, the cause of his misfortune. Yes, he had to do it in an attempt to lighten the burden of such a damning curse.

"No, Assomo, I don't have a heart of stone. But, you see, from now on it is impossible for us to live together. Haunted by my uncle's ghost, consumed by an obsessive remorse which scorches my bowels, I can't . . . ."

"Yes, we can!" she interrupts in a persuasive tone of voice. "Nothing is impossible along the path of those who love each other. In what land do you want me to take refuge, Zibi, now that the wrath of men and the wrath of gods have decreed that I belong to you? Where shall I go, alone and without you? Don't make me cry for the rest of my life, Zibi! I would be crying both over the dead body of my husband Belinga Mvondo and over the dead body of our love. Two dead bodies for one frail, female heart; that would be too much."

She began to cry. She drew nearer Zibi and placed an arm around his neck, repeating, "Dare leave me behind, Zibi! What will become of me without you? Have mercy. . . ! Have mercy . . . !"

Muffled sobs intermittantly shook her little body, and that movement imprinted on Zibi's chest the tender caresses of two breasts, drunk with love and poorly concealed beneath a dress which had been reduced to shreds. Delightful as it was, this gentle contact made the young man sick to his stomach. Thus, he suddenly stood up and, with a powerful wave of the hand, brushed the young widow aside. As for her, she too picked herself up and trudged along behind him. then, beneath the stares of night birds who served as witnesses, they both plunged into the underbrush, interlaced with gloomy shades. Without hope, they plunged forward, going somewhere, anywhere—groping their way and haphazardly breaking their own path: the path of ill-fated lovers.

III

DR. TCHUMBA'S LITTLE SNAKE

The young man was seated on a bench in the corridor which also served as a waiting room; his legs were pressed together, and his arms were wrapped around his neck like a tight-fitting sweater.

On this beautiful, sun-drenched December morning, he felt curiously cold. And just by looking at him, even the most unpracticed eye could have diagnosed the presence of some voracious beast intent upon sucking every last drop of blood from his emaciated, scabby, gooseflesh-covered body. A tapeworm, undoubtedly . . . ! The fact is: he was so thin!

As a result of sitting for such a long time, his legs had begun to fall asleep, when a silhouette in a white smock swept into the corridor like a gust of wind and disappeared into a room opposite the bench. The man's heart began to pound like an obstinate drum. At the same time a strong desire to urinate made itself felt in his bladder. After a short visit to the washroom, he returned, his bladder still full. He planted himself in front of the closed door.

Why didn't he knock?

No, he wanted to conduct himself like a peasant who was "not like all the others!" Thus, posing one hand timidly on the door, he hesitated to knock, to enter . . . . He feared that if he created a scene, they would bawl him out. He knew how irritable his city brothers could be. The least infraction on their code of manners, and there they were flying into a huff and lambasting you with all the crudest insults . . . !

He was spinning the thread of these prudent reflections, when a nurse appeared. Her arms were filled with a tray on which test tubes, phials, flasks, and various medical instruments danced like gossiping marionettes. . . .

"What corner of the bush has this fellow crawled out from — the one who's blocking the corridor that way? Son of a . . . " she muttered, her eye betraying irritation.

"Just as I thought a moment ago," the young peasant reflected indignantly. "One should always expect an unfriendly welcome at the hands of these city people. They consider themselves whiter than a white man." He had stepped aside to allow the nurse to pass, and she had then disappeared into the room, closing the door with her heel. Fifteen minutes later, she re-opened the door and invited him in . . . .

"What's your problem, young man?" inquired the doctor, who was installed behind his desk.

The young man's only response was to give him a small card.

"What's your problem, eh?" repeated the doctor, as his eyes swept across the paper.

"It's true that I don't know for certain, doctor!"

The nurse sneered derisively and burst out, "It's the same old thing all over again."

No doubt she was thinking about all those bizarre patients and their odd mannerisms. Some demand to be treated with medicines of their own choosing. Others, because they're experiencing cramps in the stomach, are astonished to receive injections in some other part of their body. Still others complain that the prescribed dosage of the medicine is insufficient to cope with their illness. And then there are those who refuse to undress in front of hospital personnel of the opposite sex.

"Take off your clothes, Ndoumna Cyriac!" the doctor ordered imperatively.

Ndoumna Cyriac nervously scratched his temples and the trunk of his body. Then, his eyes bulging with astonishment, he looked obliquely at the nurse, as if to say, "What! Undress myself in front of a woman?" he hesitated . . . . But then the doctor, who had seen may others like him, rose to his feet, approached, and scolded, "Take off your clothes, my good fellow, and be quick about it. It's almost twelve o'clock."

Ndoumna understood that there is no time for questions of modesty at the Yaounde Central Hospital. Especially when it's getting close to noon. He turned his back to the nurse, and with trembling hands he took off his shirt, his pants, and finally his underpants. Trying with little success to cover his genitals with one hand, he mounted the examining table and rather unwillingly stretched himself out at full length.

"You still don't want to tell me what your problem is, eh?" asked the doctor as he leaned over his patient.

"I really don't know, doctor, I've already told you . . . !"

"Was it simply to tell me that, Ndoumna, that you left your little village of Mfou?"

The nurse sneered again, and then she warned the patient that it was in his own best interest to explain what was wrong with him.

"It's just . . . I really don't know, miss," he stammered. "That's why I came to see the famous Doctor Tchumba. He should know, he should! Would a healthy man waste away like me?"

"No pain anywhere?" asked Dr. Tchumba.

"None, none at all!"

"Do you have good bowel movements?"

"Ah! To speak about bowel movements to a man who can't eat!"

"And at night?"

"I can't sleep, doctor. My eyelids turn to ice. Impossible to close them. And if I try to force myself to fall asleep, I wake up a few minutes later in the grip of a horrible nightmare . . . !"

"Do you drink much?"

84

"I drink; that is, I drank a lot, but since I can't drink any more, I don't drink any more . . . !"

During this rambling conversation, the flat end of the stethoscope wandered in a series of small jumps over the patient's naked chest, while the doctor's voice periodically ordered: "Breathe deeply. . . ! More deeply . . . ! Cough . . . ! Show me your tongue. Stop breathing . . . ! Breathe again . . . ! Deeply . . . ! Talk . . . !"

"What? Talk . . . ?" the patient was astonished. "and about what? At home in Mfou we don't talk like madmen! We don't talk just for the sake of talking!"

Another of the nurse's sneering laughs resounded at these words. The doctor continued his examination — a half-serious, half-amused glint in his eye. After he had finished, he walked over to a corner of the room and washed his hands.

Clambering quickly down from the examining table, Ndoumna Cyriac felt light-hearted, like a person just released from a suffocating embrace. He couldn't bear the thought of exhibiting his nudity for such a long time in front of a woman. What a painful fifteen minutes! He felt such an icy coldness in his groin that he couldn't help wondering, as he got dressed again, if his sexual powers hadn't been diminished. It's not very reassuring to undergo a medical examination when a woman's curious stare is constantly massaging your genitals.

The doctor had returned to his chair. He stared at the young patient. He noticed that the man's face twisted into morbid grimaces and that his eyes, deeply embedded in their sockets, effused an expression of madness.

Wasn't this a case of chronic insomnia in its early stages . . . ? As he asked himself this question, he finished filling out a number of laboratory examination slips and handed them to the nurse.

At the time when this story occurred, the Yaounde Central hospital was organized and administered in the following way: On the one hand, there are national class private wards and international class private wards. They are accessible to any person whose pocketbook speaks with sufficient authority. . . . On the other hand and clearly separated from them by a discriminatory esplanade, there are the public wards, which are reserved for low-level civil servants, workers, peasants, students and the unemployed. In short, for all children of the people who lack sufficient resources.

In this latter category, the Lagarde Pavilion contains six wards for which the popular coinage "paupers' quarters" is admirably suited. It's true that they are furnished in the same way as all the other wards in the hospital: metal beds and small night tables, equally metal. And, like all the others, they are cleaned daily. But each of them is unusual in the sense that it constitutes the disconcerting kind of place where men from different social backgrounds are indiscriminately thrown together.

Contrary to its name, the "paupers' quarters" didn't only cater to poor people. Guided by the simple philosophy that death reaps its harvest equally from any hospital bed, certain well-to-do patients allowed themselves to be installed in the "paupers' quarters."

For this reason, you'll see one body trembling with fever on a bare mattress and, next to it, another one delicately swathed in the gentle warmth of sheets, blankets, quilts, coverlets, and luxurious towels.

Bewildering promiscuity!

True paupers being in the majority, the perfumes of the rich are soon lost in this pigsty, where the foulest and most stagnant odors hover permanently in the air. Odors of food scraps on mouldy plates which swarm with clouds of feasting gnats. Pungent odors of overflowing bedpans which are always belatedly emptied by grumpy orderlies. Fetid and cadaverous odors of beds impregnated with urine and fecal matter and littered with filthy, soiled rags . . . . To all that, you must add the heady, oppressive vapors of cresyl and bleach, denatured alcohol and other pharmaceutical products; then, your lungs would fill with all the gusts of foul air that emanate from the "paupers' quarters."

The most agonizing drama is that new patients arrive daily from all the outpatient clinics in the area. They are admitted to the six wards of the "paupers' quarters," which all in all contain some sixty beds. And it is with a macabre irony that the problem of utilizing these beds arises, indeed, even the most conscientious doctor would be powerless to carry out his real mission . . . . Often he has no alternative but to dismiss patients who are still very sick.

In one of these rooms, a bored Ndoumna Cyriac had been languishing for eight days. He was bored not so much because of these noxious smells. No! Within these four high and painstakingly scrubbed walls, between these two glass doors and beneath a ceiling pierced by an enormous electric light bulb — tell me — what man of the people would not have been far more at ease in such a place than in his native hovel?

Yet even in the midst of all these modern comforts, Ndoumna Cyriac was bored.

During the first three days after his arrival they had taken countless test tubes of blood from him, countless stool samples, countless bottles of urine. On the fourth day, they subjected him to a spinal tap and sent him to x-ray . . . . After all these examinations, they gave him nothing more than a few tiny pills and a teaspoon of cod-liver oil, which — all things considered — merely tickled the surface of his terrible illness.

Ndoumna was disappointed. That wasn't what he had expected in setting out on his journey to see the great Dr. Tchumba at the Yaounde Central Hospital.

Each day he would sit down on one bed after another, addressing one neighor after another to confide his worries in them and to ask their advice. . . .

"Perhaps," he sometimes said to himself, "it would be better to go home and wait for death in my own village. If I die here, among strangers, what will become of my body?" They told him that prisoners from the local penitentiary take all unclaimed bodies from the morgue and dump them without ceremony in a common grave where all the stray dogs and pigs in the neighborhood go to enjoy the feast. Dying among strangers and being buried by prisoners. . . ! The very idea made him shudder. And he repeated to himself that it would be better to return to his own people, so that if he died, he might at least receive a burial befitting a man.

Followed by several nurses, the doctor entered the ward just as these thoughts were milling about in Ndoumna Cyriac's head. He opened a large dossier which had been placed on the bed and began to page through the laboratory reports. Suddenly he knit his brows; uncustomary wrinkles spread across his face. He seemed quite disappointed. One would have concluded that he was intrigued by something he had just read. For a long time, he remained pensive. Then, slowly closing the dossier, he grumbled almost in spite of himself, "Sorry, Ndoumna! You'll have to give your bed to another patient. Come see me in my office. I'll give you something to take at home."

"What!" barked Ndoumna, drawing himself up. He was visibly disconcerted. "You can't do that, doctor! Send me away from the hospital? No! Such a renowned doctor as you, you can't . . . !"

"There's no other way Ndoumna. I can't keep you in the hospital for a few intestinal worms. Go up to my office," the doctor insisted in a paternal voice. "I'll give you something for it."

"No, doctor, you can't send me away from the hospital," beseeched Ndoumna. "Look how thin I am! Would a healthy man waste away like me?"

"I see, but go up to my office anyway!" interrupted the doctor imperiously as he passed on to the next bed.

Ndoumna pleaded; he pleaded incessantly, calling out indiscriminately to nurses or patients. Then, he suddenly tore off his clothes. He no longer felt ashamed of exposing his nudity and making a spectacle of himself. Poking a finger into his protruding ribs and flaccid muscles to show how thin he had become, he bawled out, "Would a healthy man waste away like me? And they talk about a few intestinal worms! What kind of worms would make a man waste away to this point?"

Furious at seeing the doctor leave the ward, Ndoumna began shouting desperately, weeping bitterly. The eyes of all the patients were on him. Some burst out in peals of laughter, others mumbled to each other in mocking tones, and the rest, visibly affected, expressed a certain sympathy for him. From among this latter group, a patient called out to him, "How do you expect the doctor to keep you here for a few intestinal worms? You're thin, and that's obvious! But he's invited you up to his office. Perhaps he'll give you a medicine that'll cure you! You should go there right away . . . !"

Another patient, who looked older than he could possibly be, approached Ndoumna. Having taken him aside, he told him confidentially, "my child, three months ago I was here for a touch of diarrhea. And here I am back again since the day before yesterday with a cough in the bottom of my lungs. They talk about sending me to the Centre Jamot. Who knows if I haven't already got tuberculosis. . . ? And it wasn't until just now that I recalled having had a neighbor in the next bed. Ah, talk about coughing. He coughed all night long, and all day too. It was funny how he coughed and made one feel sorry for him, poor fellow . . . . Watch out; it isn't always a bed of roses to stay in these places, where all the unhealthiest breezes are blowing. For that matter, let me tell you that you never cease to amaze me! Weren't you yourself becoming impatient the other day. . . ? My child, you must realize that the white man's medicine is not capable of curing all diseases. For example, jaundice . . . . Your eyes turn yellow, completely yellow like raw palm oil. Yes, it must be jaundice that's making you so thin. And the white man's medicine can't do a thing about it. The proof is that none of the laboratory tests detected it — not in your blood, not in your stools, not in your urine. But your eyes are yellow like raw palm oil. And only a black medicine-man could cure you! Don't you have a medicine-man in your own village at Mfou . . . ?"

Ndoumna Cyriac listened with one ear to the neighbor with a cough in the bottom of his lungs. He wanted to reply that the best medicine-men in Mfou had already practiced all their cures on him . . . in vain! He wanted to explain it to his fellow patient. But, as you know, one's mouth often becomes incapable of speech when one's heart is choked with sorrow. He contented himself with a sullen scowl of vexation. But on the advice of another neighbor, he got dressed again and sat down on his bed, rolling his yellow eyes, completely yellow like raw palm oil.

Fifteen minutes later, the ward nurse re-appeared, followed by two Malabars lugging a patient who was precariously balanced on an old stretcher.

"What're you still doing here, you, the man from Mfou?" she began to scold. "The doctor told you to go see him in his office! What're you still doing here, huh? Get out of that bed, and be quick about it. This new admission is sicker than you are."

The man from Mfou got up immediately, completely abashed; he shuffled gloomily away from the "paupers' quarters."

*

*   *

The doctor was waiting for him in his office. He gave him two bottles filled with pills. After having fully explained the directions for taking each prescription, he concluded curtly, "Come back and see me again in a month!"

"Ohhh," burst out Ndoumna Cyriac. "What. . . ? A whole month . . . ? Doctor, one would think you're unaware of what could very well happen in a month . . . ? Look how thin I'm getting. Would a healthy man waste away like me? I could be dead before the month is over!"

The doctor's eyes opened wide with amazement; he stared fixedly, inquiringly at his patient. For the second time, he thought the man looked beaten. Perhaps it would be necessary to refer him to the Centre Jamot. The case would certainly be of interest to his colleague, the psychiatrist! As he followed this train of thought, he attempted to reassure the patient: "You're not so sick, Ndoumna, that you're going to die in the next month! Look: everything in your body is functioning normally — heart, lungs, liver, blood. Don't you have confidence in me?"

"How you talk; certainly I have confidence, doctor. If I hadn't had confidence, I wouldn't have come from Mfou — I wouldn't have come such a distance just to see you. I've heard so much about you! But you tell me to come back again in a month. Ohhh, a month. . . ! I'm scared, really scared . . . !"

"You're scared? Of what?"

"Of dying before the month is over. . . ! It could happen several days from now, tomorrow, even today; who knows?"

Head in hands, the patient had begun to cry once again.

This scene was neither new nor surprising to Doctor Tchumba. He had seen it many times before in all its many forms. But still he couldn't remain indifferent at the sight of tears being shed by this emaciated young peasant who was visibly obsessed with the idea of death. Nevertheless, nearly all the laboratory tests had been negative. A single one indicated the presence of *ascaridae* in Ndoumna's stomach. Like Ndoumna, the doctor seriously doubted that thread-worms alone could make a man waste away like that. He got up, walked to the door, and locked it with a double turn of the key. He returned to his desk and motioned Ndoumna into an over-stuffed chair, saying to him: "All right, listen, my friend. Now, we're all alone. Speak freely to me. What is your problem? Why are you so afraid of dying?"

*

*   *

In 1955, Ndoumna Cyriac, who was seventeen years old at the time, had just passed the examination for his *C.E.P.* * But his father died, and that had burdened him with a large inheritance and numerous responsibilities. Painful ordeal for a young man who, according to the fashionable way of judging such matters, dreamed of everything but the life of a peasant. However, little by little and with the passage of time, he got used to it.

To the great satisfaction of his poor mother, who hadn't had any other children, and to the great satisfaction of the entire tribe, Ndoumna proved equal to his new responsibilities. He worked hard in the cocoa plantation and in the vegetable gardens. Fathers and mothers often cited him as a good example, when they needed to scold their own lazy children: "Don't you see Ndoumna, the only son of the late Olama . . . ? A poor orphan no older than you! But he's already proving to everyone that his father's *elig*** is occupied by the son of a true man! Die of shame for being unable to make yourself useful to the country, like him!"

Making one's self useful to one's country. . . ! Ndoumna Cyriac thought of nothing else until a time, four years later, when a former classmate, Essomba Joachim, returned to the village.

Essomba Joachim had obtained his C.E.P. at the same time as Ndoumna Cyriac. But as for him, he had passed a civil service examination two years later and, as a result, had been received into the ranks of Customs Inspectors. From that moment on, a yawning chasm had separated the two young men. And also from that moment on, Essomba Joachim had become more educated, more experienced, and more wealthy than Ndoumna. Yes, indisputably wealthier with suitcases, trunks, a metal bed, a gas lamp, a motorbike, and furniture not to be found anywhere else in the entire region, and then too he had an *nguelmafom.**** Oh, an *nguelmafom*, that says everything! Essomba Joachim had one.

---

*Certificat d'Etudes Primaires (School-Leaving Certificate), roughly equivalent to a high-school diploma.

**estate bequeathed by an illustrious man

***deformation of English "gramophone"

An *nguelmafom* . . . ! Just think of the excitement that it had created in Mfou during the young civil servant's three-month vacation. In his father's *abaa*, it was one continuous party. All the villagers flocked there, and they were filled with respect. Above all, they wanted to hear an *nguelmafom* for the first time. . . ! One record, then another, and another, and another! Without interruption and amidst thunderous bursts of laughter, which were washed down with ample swigs of palm wine.

Essomba Joachim's prestige had been firmly established; he had just succeeded in eclipsing everyone else. For once, the good and evil tongues of Mfou were unanimous. "The son of Mbida Essomba," they repeated, "is a great man. He has brought us an *nguelmafom* from the city; he has brought us the white man's speaking box in which the voices of dead people are buzzing away!"

What added a certain touch to this enormous and rather noisy prestige was the fact that, on returning to his post, he had left behind a small house coquettishly coifed with a sheet metal roof, the first and only one to have sprouted from the soil of Mfou . . . !"

How could Ndoumna Cyriac help being tormented by evil thoughts? No, the inequality which now existed between himself and his former classmate was totally unjustifiable, especially since the latter had never been better than him in school. Isn't there somebody on this earth capable of giving a true man's stature to those who crawl on their bellies? To this unsettling question, a widespread rumor one day discreetly answered "yes."

As a matter of fact, for some time the local "word-of-mouth" network had been announcing that a mysterious guest was staying at the home of the wealthy planter Mbassi. Mysterious, because people knew very little about him. His name was Samnick. He was Bassa. He could make a man's happiness.

Samnick had already uncovered the cause of the *bibolo** with which Mbassi's huge cocoa plantation had until then been plagued: a small canary filled with onion-fetishes and hidden beneath a bush by some enemy. It was Mbassi himself who spread this piece of news. To anyone willing to listen, he claimed that Samnick had done this, that Samnick had done that, and that he was capable of doing many other things as well! In short, the wealthy planter Mbassi enthusiastically attributed all sorts of good things to the mysterious Samnick.

Samnick . . . , there was the man Ndoumna Cyriac had been dreaming about — Ndoumna Cyriac who had become passionately desirous of eliminating the revolting difference which relegated him to a place far below that of his former classmate.

In the manner of all those who know how to read the past and the future of men, Samnick, when consulted, emitted an enormous burst of eloquent laughter. As far as he was concerned, Ndoumna was merely suffering from a benign concern: the desire to be rich. He felt obligated to demonstrate the magic powers invested in him. At his demand, a basin was filled with herbs and water. He asked for a 100 franc bill, which he threw into the water. He covered the basin with a red cloth; then he mumbled a few magic words and executed several impressive sleights of hand. He removed the cloth and

---

*a sporous blight of the cocoa plant, commonly known as "brown rot"

ordered Ndoumna to empty the receptacle. Amazement filled the spectators when he retreived a 1,000 franc bill from among the herbs!

"Keep it for yourself, Ndoumna," says Samnick in a generous tone of voice. Having drawn the young man aside, he whispers in his ear, "You know, since I'm not always around, there is a way to make you a talisman capable of . . . . To tell the truth, I only offer it to souls chosen by my *minkuk*.* And you are one of them! The price, rest assured, will not exceed 50,000 francs. For you, of course!"

How can you explain it? That a man capable of miraculously producing money to assure the happiness of his fellow-creatures could nevertheless be asking for money? "Pay me money, so that I can make money for you!" Truly, it was incomprehensible! Probably Ndoumna Cyriac understood something about it.

He was engaged. In anticipation of the dowry to be paid for the young woman, his mother was hoarding 60,000 honestly and laboriously accumulated francs at the back of a granary. To ferret these precious savings from their sombre hiding place, the young man had recourse to all the subterfuges hidden in the depths of the human mind — lies, preposterous tales, and deceptions — which taken together constitute what people are in the habit of calling intelligence.

But you know, when a mother plays the role of banker, she plays it magnificently. Not a single sou is removed from the pile without a long and difficult explanation. Thus Ndoumna explained himself at length and with difficulty . . . . What does he say to his mother, who doesn't even want to hear the famous Samnick mentioned? No one will ever know! But the fact remains that, at the cost of wry faces, fasts, fits of sulking, grumblings and angry silences, a sum of 50,000 francs finally moved out of the maternal granary several days later.

"Don't kill me, my son; here's your money . . . !" exclaimed the poor women, her eye dark with anger as she reluctantly threw a tidy little packet on the floor at his feet.

As agreed, Ndoumna leaves home at the first crowing of the cocks to knock on Samnick's door. It opens on a mystifying scene: a room illuminated by countless candles. In the background of this strange world is a figure dressed in a long, red robe and wearing a turban of the same color. What perfumes floating above all that? One would almost say that a thousand sweet-smelling flowers were sending forth vapors from all their pores. The door securely locked from the inside, Samnick first observes his young client; his eyes are like those of a snake hypnotizing its victim before striking; then he mutters suddenly, "I will make you swallow a little snake which. . . ."

He doesn't have time to finish his sentence. Suddenly overcome by an uncontrollable fit of trembling, Ndoumna Cyriac starts in fright and utters a horrified cry. Swallow what . . . ? A proposal as unexpected and unbelievable as it was macabre!

"A s-s-snake! Swal-low a s-s-snake . . . !" he manages to mumble almost unconsciously, as he makes the sign of the cross. "If I had only known. . . !"

He raised both hands to his head as if to exert all his strength in arresting the flight

---

*a gnome or totemic animal

of his reason. which seemed to be vaporizing. Dumbfounded, he railed against Nature, "Why," he said to himself, "why didn't Nature give men wings? Yes, wings . . . ! How often man succumbs to danger for the simple reason that he wasn't endowed at birth with wings!"

Seeing the young man's entire body tremble, Samnick whispers in a distant voice, "People might almost say that you're afraid, my child. . . . You'd be making a mistake. You won't be the first to swallow a little magic snake! Besides, it's too late to turn back, since the whole thing has already been set in motion. And if you refuse to go through with it now, watch out for the fury of my *minkuk*!"

Turn back. . . ? Refuse . . .? Ndoumna was no longer capable of that. Not only because the fury of a *minkuk* is terrifying, but also because the young peasant already saw (with the eyes of his subconscious) wads and wads of banknotes piling up behind his 50,000 francs. How could he turn back from that which he had coveted for such a long time? He only had to take one more step in order to have it. He would become rich; not only rich, but richer than his former classmate, the Customs Inspector Essomba Joachim! And then, among other things, he'd buy an *nguelmafom*. And he'd be respected throughout the region, and he'd prove to everyone that his father's *elig* was occupied by the son of a true man . . . !

The prospect was marvelous. It instantly cured Ndoumna of the shameless fear which had been toying with him just a moment ago. He reflected that he was a person of the male sex and that a person of the male sex didn't have the right to tremble like a woman. Yes, indeed! But before long, the fear, which was stronger than he was, returned to the attack, when Samnick approached and began to tighten a blindfold over his eyes, muttering in a religious tone of voice, "This way you'll no longer be afraid, my child. Tell yoruself that if men had no eyes, they'd never be afraid of anything; they'd master the universe, and the path of progress would be wide open . . . ! True courage, my child, can only be found in people who know how to close their eyes to the traps and dangers with which daily life is teeming! And human happiness is bought at that price — taking risks with one's eyes closed! Don't be afraid then, my child; grit your teeth! Life belongs to those who fend for themselves . . . !"

Ndoumna Cyriac gritted his teeth and allowed his eyes to be blindfolded. Yet all those reassuring words reached him as if from a world he no longer inhabited. His legs had begun to shake again. Soaked with sweat, his body itched strangely. His head weighed so heavily that he asked himself if it hadn't become as large as a mountain.

Samnick's momentary silence gave him the impression that he had been abandoned in a universe populated with evil spirits. It gave him the feeling of a dreadful loneliness. Muffled sounds, muted sounds, sounds like tinkling crystal. . . . What in the world could Samnick have been doing amidst all those less than reassuring sounds? Suddenly Ndoumna started with unspeakable terror as a ghost-like hand unexpectedly grabbed his head and tilted it backwards, while a voice, which he no longer recognized as that of Samnick, commanded him to open his mouth and swallow. . . . Frozen with fear, Ndoumna fainted.

On regaining consciousness, he saw himself stretched out on a mat. He was feeling the same fatigue one feels after a long, drawn-out brawl. He examined his body to see if it had sustained any wounds. What had Samnick, who was sitting calmly on the bed, done to him. . . ? His belly replied to the question. It replied with an unusual rumbling . . . . That was when Ndoumna became afraid of his belly! Afraid to know that from then on, a small magic snake would be there. He got up as if to run away from himself. Trembling, he sat down next to Samnick.

"Don't be afraid," Samnick repeated. "You were so brave, my child! Why be afraid now that the whole operation has proceeded under favorable circumstances. . . ? You'll only have to place nine chicken eggs under your bed on the night of a full moon, and the next day you'll do no more than stretch out your hand to gather up — guess what? Wads and wads of banknotes . . . ! But the magic will only begin to take effect in three months. Between now and then, relax, because this has been very tiring!"

What . . . ? In three what . . . ? Oh! What a long time! Who knows what can happen in three months?

Meanwhile, it's true, after having been lavishly entertained by all his customers, Samnick leaves the village of Mfou under the pretext of having received urgent invitations from some other place.

The brave Ndoumna laboriously begins counting the days, counting the days and the weeks, counting the weeks and the months . . . . One day, two, three, that's it . . . ! On the night of a full moon, he locks himself in his room earlier than usual. He carefully places nine fresh chicken eggs beneath his bed; then he lies down, his heart drumming with hope. He eats nothing that evening — what's the purpose of eating when one is expecting to get rich?

Troubled by this premature going to bed, his mother — poor woman — comes knocking at the door. She asks why this and why that? Above all she wants to know if her only son, her beloved Ndoumna, is sick . . . . Bah, poor honest mothers of the world, no one will ever know the flames of love and anguish which sear your hearts in the presence of your suffering children . . . ! As for being ill, Ndoumna was seriously ill.

With the strength of his thoughts, rigid as an iron bar, he flogged the night like an overly anxious rider beating his horse.

He wanted the day to arrive before it was due. The soft moonlight formed a terrible screen between the present, which weighed heavily on him, and the future, which he desired to possess and live to its fullest extent. However, blameless night flowed along at its same measured and time-honored pace, ultimately giving birth in all innocence to a beautiful golden morning greeted by all the cocks of Mfou.

Eyes red with sleeplessness, Ndoumna Cyriac jumps nimbly from bed and utters a sigh of relief. After stretching himself and smiling a blissful smile, he lowers himself and energetically plants one knee on the ground; then he extends a greedy, trembling hand beneath the bed. Alas, the hand encounters nothing more than the ironic surfaces of nine fresh chicken eggs! O God of poor people . . . !

Many days and many weeks pass, and no one bothers to count them. Two months later, Ndoumna can't explain to anyone why he is wasting away. Consumed with worry and anguish, the handsome and highly enterprising young man of just a short time ago is losing his flesh before one's very eyes and shriveling into a depressing silence. He is always accompanied by an inexorable fatigue. Attending to his daily chores becomes impossible for him. All day long, he can be seen sitting or lying down in his mother's cramped little kitchen. During the night, an oppressive anxiety tortures his soul and keeps his eyes perpetually open.

At first, many inhabitants of Mfou take the whole thing as a joke. They are amused and think Ndoumna has been stricken by *sunuk,** that benign malady which plagues every adolescent who rounds the cape of puberty. Whenever Ndoumna goes by, they smile, they laugh, they sneer, they smirk and whisper, "What woman has smitten our good Ndoumna with *sunuk*? Who can she be?" But in the face of the young man's abnormal loss of weight, they are soon obliged to reconsider. No, the *sunuk* doesn't carry its jokes to the point where bones emerge and eyes sink back into their sockets, no! It's at this time that people decide to mobilize all the best medicine-men of Mfou. . . ! In vain.

Then one day, several members of the tribe return from the city. Struck by the deplorable condition of Ndoumna, they waste no time in spreading a sensational piece of news! "A black man, a true son of the people has just returned from France, armed with all the white man's diplomas . . . ! He comes right out of the largest school in Paris; and his medicine — all intact and still warm — is producing genuine miracles at the Yaounde Central Hospital . . . ! Next to him, all the other doctors are thrust into the shadows; one might almost say that they've just forgotten their profession . . . . And every day the new doctor is besieged by sick people flocking to him from all corners of the country. . . !"

His skin clinging to his bones and tortured by the conviction that he is harboring a dangerous young snake in his bowels, Ndoumna Cyriac laboriously drags himself without further delay to the Yaounde Central Hospital in order to see — nothing more than to see with his own eyes, yellow as raw palm oil — that illustrious black doctor about whom the entire country had so much to say.

"There it is, doctor, the secret of my illness. I couldn't reveal it to anyone but you alone. I know that you're a great doctor and that you won't deceive me. And I know that you, and you alone, can get rid of this wretched little snake for me . . . ! You can do it, doctor!"

With eyes and ears wide open, Doctor Tchumba had listened to this strange adventure with the witch-doctor Samnick. He heaved a profound sigh of relief, as if his momentarily blocked lungs had suddenly begun to function again.

"Yes, yes, I can do it!" he affirmed as if speaking to someone else. "But what did the little snake look like?"

"A very small snake colored. . . colored black! With a little red tongue like a flame

---

*anemia and emaciation which the Beti commonly interpret as a consequence of one's first sexual experience.

of fire! With. . . with . . . in fact it was probably a young viper! I was so afraid to look at it.

Doctor Tchumba got up. As he went to open the door again, he casually said, "very well . . . . Come see us again in three days . . . ! That will give me time to prepare a medicine that isn't carried by any pharmacy in Cameroon."

*

*   *

As punctual as the totemic panther on the appointed day, Ndoumna Cyriac was sitting on the patients' bench long before the working day began. As he entered the corridor, Dr. Tchumba recognized him among the crowd of people waiting there. A look of wonderment like a halo of well-being floated above his emaciated face. It resembled the face of a prisoner who knows that an order for his immediate release is being prepared. His heart was throbbing, no longer with fear and anxiety, but with that sweet anguish which sometimes takes hold of us on the threshold of an anticipated but as yet unattained happiness. Dr. Tchumba led Ndoumna by the hand into his office, telling him in a kindly voice, "Don't be afraid, my friend. It won't take long."

If Dr. Tchumba only knew . . . ! His patient couldn't possibly have been afraid of him. On the contrary, he was in a hurry to rid himself of a fatal burden, the menacing presence of which he felt in his guts, in his veins, in his muscles, in his very soul. Thus, he was gazing at Dr. Tchumba the way one gazes at a savior.

Making the sign of the cross, he installed himself in a chair; then he (once again!) submissively allowed his eyes to be blindfolded. In the darkness behind his new blindfold, he noticed that his legs were no longer trembling, as in the witch-doctor Samnick's room, and that his head was not as big as a mountain. It is because he had confidence. Every sound told him that the moment of his deliverance was approaching. However that might be, he speculated for an instant: was the doctor going to cut open his stomach? It was fascinating — the sound of a scissors against a large, open-mouthed jar! And he actually heard it against a background of muffled whisperings. And then, the bitter odor of ethyl alcohol permeating his senses. . . ! Was the doctor going to cut open his stomach? What difference did it make! He had confidence. And because he had confidence, Ndoumna Cyriac remained prudently calm during a quarter hour filled as much with anxiety as with hope.

"Drink this medicine," the doctor commanded. "After that, lower your head and keep your mouth wide open. Have confidence. It won't take long."

"I have confidence, a great deal of confidence," echoed Ndoumna in a muted voice. "Save me! You can do it, doctor."

The medicine was a spoonful of liquid. Ndoumna swallowed it, and he felt a curious shiver pass through his entire body. His heart contracted and dilated, contracted and dilated. Almost as if an enormous abdominal muscle had become detached from its deep-lying roots. His mouth filled with a bitter-tasting saliva. Like an octopus extending its tentacles, an all-embracing weariness took hold of him. At the same time, his eyes were overcome by dizziness. He had the painful sensation of falling, falling freely, falling endlessly into one of those bottomless pits one only sees in dreams. But because he had confidence, Ndoumna knew he wasn't lost, couldn't be lost as long as he was in Dr. Tchumba's hands.

The latter and his nurse were standing on either side of him, gently but firmly immobilizing his shoulders and his head. The patient himself was motionless. His mouth wide open and directed toward the washbasin, he remained as docile and obedient as a sheep being milked. All of a sudden, convulsions shook his ribs, nausea ate into his heart, his intestines, his stomach. . . . A salvo of hiccoughs erupted from his chest, and finally: "Uuuwaaak! Uuuwaaak! Uuuwaaak!"

At that moment the nurse quickly snatched a large, open-mouthed jar from the table; it bore the identifying inscription: "Nkolbisson Agriculture Center." With that dexterity of fingers which were accustomed to manipulating fragile objects, she quickly opened it and emptied its contents into the washbasin.

"That's it!" burst out the doctor triumphantly.

As soon as Ndoumna's eyes were uncovered, he cast a curiously savage glance into the washbasin. How astonished he was to see a snake, a tiny little snake gamboling madly about in his vomit. He couldn't contain himself for joy. He felt waves of new-found health coursing violently through his veins, and as he fell to his knees, he cried out, "That's it, doctor, the little snake that was on the verge of bringing me to an untimely end."

After having kissed Dr. Tchumba's shoes with the tip of his tongue, he got up and reflected for some time, while next to him the nurse was doubled over with laughter. Ndoumna thought she was sharing in his joy. Thus, laughing like a madman, he turned around and embraced her, but she burst out in horrified screams, exerting her feeble womanly powers to the utmost in defending herself from him. She heaped insults on the ill-mannered patient: "imbecile, brute, rogue, let go of me!" Visibly disappointed, Ndoumna stepped back and turned to the person he regarded as a savior.

"What do you intend to do with this dangerous little snake, doctor?" he inquired in a confidential tone.

"Why do you ask?" sighed the doctor, a sanctimonious smile on his lips.

First, Ndoumna coughed vigorously. Then, gesturing expansively with his arms, he barked at the top of his lungs, "Doctor, I would advise you to burn it alive! That way the witch-doctor Samnick and his evil little snakes will perish forever from this earth . . . to the great good fortune of all mankind!"

IV

OLD MBARTA'S TWO DAUGHTERS

In African society, it would be unthinkable for an old man with two young daughters to languish in poverty and solitude. Especially when a witch-doctor who hurls lightning bolts becomes involved.

If you could only have seen him two years ago in the village of Kondo-Biback. . . ! If you could only have seen him, you certainly wouldn't have been able to prevent yourself from laughing at him, as everyone else was doing at that time; and, like everyone else, you wouldn't have been able to prevent yourself from feeling sorry for him in his misery.

He was hardly ever seen by day. He arose with the first chirpings of the birds, disappeared into the bush, and didn't return until the last rays of daylight were playing over the village.

Men never hesitate to attribute madness to people who fail to adopt their own customs and habits. Thus, it is not surprising that nearly all the inhabitants of Kondo-Biback regarded this solitary and mysterious old man as somewhat touched in the head. And out loud they laughed at him, although beneath their laughter, they felt pity.

But as for him, he often surprised them. He surprised them with reflections which could hardly come from the head of a man who had lost his faculties. To a group of youthful enthusiasts who were boasting about their wealth, their agility, and the strength of their muscles while mockingly threatening to beat him up, he dedicated this improvised refrain, which he hummed to the accompaniment of his little *mvet:*

> za alod ma avë . . . ?
> mot alod makuma
> mâ melod nye a me bua
> mot alod ma antyë
> mâ melod nye étunn
> mot alod ma angul
> mâ melod nye ateg
> mot alod ma andomann

mâ melod nye ayom
za alod ma avë. . . ?

who outstrips me and in what. . . ?
this one richer than me
me poorer than him
that one taller than me
me shorter than him
this one stronger than me
me weaker than him
this one younger than me
me older than him
who outstrips me and in what. . . ?

The people burst out laughing, although their consciences stirred restlessly beneath the weight of these simple but original words that expressed a whole philosophy of life.

Another time, several young people, intrigued by the obscurity of his daily routine, called out to him. Mockingly they inquired whether he was the night owls' permanent guest. He replied: "My child, am I still a human being? Am I? Where have you ever seen living people fraternizing with dead ones? Am I not a dead man still on his feet? Ah, if you only knew . . . . The silent shades of the underbrush suit me better than the noisy glare of this village on the edge of the highway. If I stayed here, I would be bickering all day long with God-in-Heaven as I watched the true living become drunk with life in the bright sunshine! The sun shone upon my days, and now God-in-Heaven has extinguished it. His goodness is inscrutable . . . ! Do you want me to bicker all day long with God-in-Heaven? No, that I'll never do. Overtaken by calamity, the wise man retires from the everyday world to be reborn and to develop in his own world. Ah, if you only knew, my children, what Mbarta Kombo once was at Bilig!"

Saying this, the old man's voice became almost choked with tears.

*

*   *

Morally and physically, Mbarta Kombo represented the pale human remains from the "good old days" of the colonial period. Rich, handsome and full of vigor at the time, he stood out among those whom public opinion respectfully called *karigori*.*

These *karigori* could be recognized by their ample cotton pagnes, which tied at the hip and allowed an ankle-length fold of cloth to drape arrogantly down the sides of each leg; they could also be recognized by their heavy shirts with shoulder boards—

---

*deformation of the French "catégorie" used locally in referring to important personages and wealthy planters inscribed in a special "category" on the French colonial tax rolls.

shirts which were glued to their skins beneath military jackets they almost never took off, even during the most suffocating heat spells of the *esseb** . . . . All that majestically topped by a broad-brimmed hat or by an antiquated colonial pith helmet.

To become a *karigori*, however, it was not enough for the suppliant to be dressed in this way. It was also necessary to be recognized as a rich man living on a grand scale, even if one wasn't actually rich. The procedure usually culminated in a public show of bravado. It consisted of protesting to His Honor, the White-Commandant-on-Tour, and in front of the entire assembled local population — of indignantly protesting to see one's own name on the same tax roll as those of all the lower-class riff raff in the village. The protest was always favorably received, and the successful suppliant was delighted to pay the State three, if not four, times as much as the sum that would normally have been levied against his annual revenues.

It was by this only slightly ridiculous path that Mbarta entered, solemnly and on firm footing, into the *karigori* caste.

And like all *karigori*, he had had the honor of being feared by his relatives, loved by the women and respected by the indigenous agents of the colonial administration. No one could say that he didn't deserve this triple honor. As far as such matters were concerned, he possessed a number of assets. A cocoa plantation with over two thousand adult trees . . . ! A harem with ten women . . . ! Dozens of sheep and pigs; legions of chickens and ducks . . . ! Everything one needed to bear with dignity that noble title of *karigori*. Besides that, there were the visitors who kept coming back to make oral contributions to his prestige; then, there were the "humble servants" who came from nobody knows where and settled in the shade of his illustrious name the way ferns have the habit of growing up in the shadow of a baobab tree.

*

*   *

At the moment when the drums of national independence hurled their unprecedented exaltations to the four winds, almost nothing remained of all this wealth. Nothing but a starveling cocoa plantation invaded by mistletoe and *bibolo*; nothing but two silently dreaming houses; nothing but one skeletal dog; nothing but a single wife rapt in melancholy and the mother of two daughters. . . .

The cause of this fatal degeneration was perfectly explicable. In the first place, there were the parties he frequently gave with an eye to consolidating his prestige. Mercilessly his guests had devoured his chickens, his sheep and all the money that accrued from the sale of his cocoa. Then, there was death. It had snatched away three of his wives. Then, too there was kidnapping, so practical and so frequent in the region. It had appropriated another six of them. . . . Alas, every legal proceeding to recover them had proved fruitless. Sometimes, in responding to the summons of the court, the putative accomplices came only to deny and to advise Mbarta to seek his unfaithful wives elsewhere. Sometimes, out of pure and simple respect for the administrative authorities, the errant wives themselves appeared and falsely promised to return home.

---

*the long rainy season in Cameroon (December-March)

Yes, only a single wife remained to him at the moment when the drums of national independence bellowed forth their unprecedented exaltations to the four winds! It was the one whose name was Atizi. You ask yourself what could possibly retain Atizi a little while longer in the compound of a husband who was always aggressively stuffed into his old, ill-fitting military jacket of a *karigori*. And immediately you think of a wife's love for her husband . . . ! But no, women who continued to tolerate senseless cruelties had become exceedingly rare at that decisive moment in history, and Atizi was not one of them. Everyone knows that a woman's heart resides where her children can be found. And that was the reason why Atizi, the only mother in Mbarta's harem, had chosen to remain a little while longer.

Everywhere the death-rattles of a dying era resounded, while at the same time the triumphant wails of another one in the throes of birth were screeching through the air. Everywhere an unseasonable wind was blowing . . . outraging the most sacred traditions of the land, smashing the most solidly established privileges, overturning the habits most solidly rooted in the customs of the people. To everyone, regardless of sex, the new dawn brought the enjoyment of equal civil liberties. A woman, for example, would henceforth have the right to follow her own taste in the choice of a husband, or, as the case may be, to abandon the one her parents had imposed upon her when, completely naive and defenseless, she knew but a single liberty — uncomplaining submission to the will of others.

For the older luminaries of the area, this official hurly-burly opened the door upon an intolerable world. It was a scandal, an unprecedented sacrilege. The black man had difficulty conceiving that a woman could enjoy the same stature and importance as himself in human society . . . . A woman was his pleasure machine; a woman was his agricultural machine; a woman was, finally, something he had bought in the same way one buys a beast of burden!

However, the wheel of history continued to turn. In vain men stared, brandished whips, and tortured their partners-for-life in every possible way, but each day they saw their millennial authority crumbling irrevocably. It was like a house in which the main beam was being gnawed away by termites. And women, liberated from a long night of slavery, felt their wings spreading out, and they didn't hesitate to swagger a bit. And one could hear them humming in mocking voices:

> minlan mi okoba mimann ya. . . !
> mot abad me fogo
> *meyelë* a pa-ba-ba
> anë ndelë-ononn!. . .

> Gone are the blahs of former times.
> If someone touches me now
> Frrrt. . . ! I fly away
> like a swallow . . . .

To tell the truth, the men saw themselves caught in an hopeless quagmire. The wisest ones timidly adapted themselves to the pace of history. They ranted and raved under their breath; they swore in half-finished curses, and they mistreated their wives with half-completed gestures. And beneath the marital roof, life continued to plod more or less successfully along its usual path.

However, the prestigious *karigori* of Bilig had the misfortune of being born into the hereditary line of those who firmly believed that Africa—the Africa of their day—dared no longer move one step in any direction. Like an old palm tree in the rock garden, Mbarta remained fanatically rooted in traditional custom. Swollen with illusions, he persisted in showing himself to be authoritarian, brutal, and rather unsociable.

In his concession, which had been reduced to two ramshackle huts, he woke up one day; his ears were filled with a disconcerting silence—a silence as disconcerting as the bad dreams which plagued his slumbers from that moment on. Atizi, the only one still under his heel, and her two daughters had fled during the night. Like his other wives, they had flown away to seek the remembrance of time past.

*
*   *

Anyone else but Mbarta Kombo would have decided to move out. But he had remained, as people say, alone. Alone with his heart, alone with his skeletal dog, alone with his little *mvet* which, in addition to several rare visitors, had become the sole companion of his conversations.

Yet solitude is hardly suitable to advanced age. Especially in a lost corner of the bush, far removed from society. It was unsettling. Members of the tribe no longer came to Bilig except to convince Mbarta to do as they had done — to abandon this ancient village where they had all been born and (as they had done) to install himself at Kondo-Biback on the edge of the highway. But there was a difficulty, you see, because certain places become part of a man's being, simply by the fact of his having lived there.

Every tree in Bilig seemed to be covered with skin from Mbarta's hands and nourished with sweat and blood from Mbarta's body. All the birds in the trees seemed to chant the name "Mbarta" and to build their nests there solely to remain near Mbarta. At the thought of leaving that mystical little family, what sorrow. . . !

One day when his cousin Abena had come to visit him, he was found in bed, painfully afflicted with boils. Without asking Mbarta's permission, Abena went back to Kondo-Biback. Shortly afterwards he returned with many other members of the tribe. They transported the old recluse to the hospital. Two weeks later, as soon as he arose from his sick-bed, Mbarta spoke only about returning to Bilig.

"No, no, Mbarta! You can no longer go back to Bilig! You see, if you had died, your blood would have been upon our heads! No, you can no longer go back to Bilig."

Every voice in Kondo-Biback was unanimous. Vanquished by the law of numbers, Mbarta too became resigned. He installed himself among his people, no longer to soar the heights as he had during the good old days of the *karigori*, but to crawl on his belly.

*
*   *

Mbarta Kombo chose a site. In a spirit of solidarity, every arm in Kondo-Biback helped to erect a building there. It was a very small one-room hut on the outskirts of the village. Late into the night, melancholy harmonies could still be heard filtering out of this minuscule lodging as a little *mvet* and a tear-filled voice intoned their impromptu melodies.

To be sure, traditional hospitality placed every dish of food in the village at Mbarta's disposal. But a man who has lived an independent existence doesn't easily adjust to being received everywhere as if we were a parasite. Previously he had always eaten what he wanted. Now he was eating what others wanted! Besides, he eventually came to suspect that they sometimes made fun of him behind his back, so he deprived his stomach of these meals with fixed menus. He decided never again to set foot in anyone else's hut.

No one ever really succeeded in convincing him to reconsider his decision. Nevertheless, the inhabitants of Kondo-Biback could not tolerate for long that this old man, the father of two daughters, should vegetate in solitude and poverty. The village elders decreed that Atouba and Nanga be obliged to return. They were living with their mother, that unfaithful woman, in a village located some two or three river-crossings from Kondo-Biback. When informed of this project, even though it would have been in his own best interest, Mbarta merely smiled. He objected by coining a witticism "Nge mot abenn wa, woligi nye ebenn. If someone turns you down, help him turn you down."

Bah, the absurd sophistries of a painfully embittered old man! People disregard them, and one fine morning four young men disappear from the village and return in the evening with the two turtledoves in tow.

Everyone welcomed the event with great enthusiasm. Including Mbarta Kombo himself. But wagging tongues pass an unfavorable judgment on the two young women. Their father wallowing in misery, while they are still in the same neighborhood! Not even wanting to help him! One of them is seventeen and the other fifteen. Young women of that age are certainly capable of attending to someone else's needs. Their ears are stuffed with counsels and threats, but they are also mollified with a few culinary delicacies. . . .

Atouba and Nanga explain themselves. They shift the entire burden of responsibility for their misconduct onto their mother Atizi, who (they insist) threatened to beat them every time they expressed a desire to visit their father.

An easy way out and as good as any other for pleading their cause! As an old proverb says, "the mouth never runs out of reasons." Indeed, one month later, after having lulled the townspeople's vigilance to sleep by their deceptively docile attitudes, Atouba and Nanga disappear.

For the second time, a group of young people go out to dislodge them from their nest. And for the second time, the two turtledoves, irresistably attracted by maternal authority, fly away from Kondo-Biback.

When they are brought back for the third time, their hands are securely tied behind their backs. First, they are subjected to a good flogging; then, it becomes necessary to employ the services of a witch-doctor.

The witch-doctor prescribes a *sab*,* and without delay the villagers disrobe the two sisters, who are crying and shouting at the top of their lungs. But their calls of distress move none of the bystanders to pity. Fingernails and toenails, eye lashes and eyebrows are clipped . . . . A lock of hair is cut from the head and tufts of hair from under the armpits and between the legs. A few drops of blood are exacted from them, and then, having mixed all these bodily contributions with chunks of coal, the witch-doctor fashions a parcel, which he buries in the courtyard while reciting a few obscure incantations. Then, having turned toward the two victims, who are dazed and inundated with tears, he roars in a menacing voice: "Run away again, my little disobedient ones! For it is no longer with your father that you will have to settle accounts, but with the dreadful God *Zēyang*** . . . !"

Atouba and Nanga emit the terror-filled screeches of cornered animals. They struggle desperately, rolling on the ground at their father's feet. Perish by lightning. . . ? The very thought drives them out of their minds with fear.

"Oh, father! Oh, father! Would you leave us to the mercy of someone who hurls lightning bolts? Oh, father, have you forgotten that we are your own flesh and blood? Oh, father, don't abandon us!"

A number of nearby voices shout menacingly: "Close your little beaks, filled to overflowing with hypocrisies! Close them! If not, another flogging! Don't make fun of Mbarta any more. It's today that you seem to understand for the first time that you are the blood of his blood. A thousand tombs . . . ! And you who permitted him to wallow in misery for such a long time . . . !"

The two young women remain silent. But their tears continue to flow in profusion. Their two pairs of hands gesture imploringly in the direction of their old father.

Seated on a log in the corner, he is nervously chewing kola nuts, his eye darkened with an aura of mystery. Suddenly, he gets up and indignantly bellows in his cavernous voice:

"It is to you that I address myself, all of you who are present here, my brothers and my children, my sisters and my daughters! I'm convinced, I'm firmly convinced that you came to Bilig and routed me from my little nest there in order to kill me! Yes, and today I see the proof of it . . . ! Do you know what children represent for any man? The heart of his heart, yes. . . . If you only knew! Whatever their crime might be, how do you dare amuse yourselves in this way with the lives of Atouba and Nanga? After all, they are the blood of my blood! No, truly you have no idea how all this is breaking my heart. . . !"

---

*the practice of collecting bodily excretions, blood, fingernails, toenails, and hair from people in order to cast a spell on them.

**Lightning, personified in Cameroonian mythology as a terrifying divinity.

Whispered complaints and muted protests rise from the astounded assembly. . . .

Scorning his advanced age, young people heap all the most disparaging epithets upon Mbarta. Between two salvos of handclapping, women take no pains to conceal their disapproval and disappointment.

They grumble, accusing Mbarta of wanting to banish their mouths from the opportunity of ever eating sow's meat at his daughters' weddings. After having guarded their tongues and stared in wide-eyed amazement for a long time, the village elders confess that Mbarta's attitude is totally incomprehensible to them.

Whereupon the witch-doctor imposes silence on the whole group; then, he gives one and all to understand that the dreadful God *Zéyang* is already suspended above the head of Atouba, Nanga, and anyone else in Kondo-Biback who would venture to. . . ."

The witch-doctor leaves his awe-struck listeners to finish his fateful prophecy. Which means he doesn't fool around, not him!

*

*   *

Restrained from then on by the superstitious fear of seeing themselves reduced to ashes by a flash of lightning, Atouba and Nanga no longer dared run away from Kondo-Biback. Papa Mbarta's hut outgrew its minuscule dimensions and shabby appearance. It became joyful and donned a new hat in the form of a corrugated metal roof.

If you could only have seen him two years ago . . . ! Old Mbarta certainly was a pitiful sight. Today, it's a rare vehicle which doesn't stop at his door to disgorge unexpected visitors, bearers of no less unexpected gifts. It's just that poverty and solitude in an old man, father of two daughters, are quite unthinkable in African society.

Yes, thanks to a witch-doctor who hurls lightning bolts, old Mbarta and his two daughters are living happily together these days. But it can also be said that, on account of old Mbarta's two daughters, the people of Kondo-Biback are also living in terror these days. There is nobody who doesn't know that *Zéyang* is a god who is blind! Indeed, people had seen him breathe his fatal fire on just about anybody at a time when a powerful witch-doctor had directed him elsewhere by remote control! Thus, every time the Sky puts on a sad face and emits rumblings from its mysterious belly, every heart in Kondo-Biback palpitates with fear and anguish.

As you know, there is no greater martyrdom than living with constantly jangled nerves. That's why all the inhabitants of Kondo-Biback agreed to exorcise the menace hanging over their heads. To do that, however, it would be necessary to unearth the magic parcel and neutralize the terrifying powers of the lightning bolt. But where is the witch-doctor, the only one qualified to initiate such occult proceedings? They're still looking for him. . . .

In the meantime, every heart in Kondo-Biback continues to palpitate with fear and anguish every time the Sky puts on a sad face and emits the least rumbling from its mysterious belly.

104

V

THE SANGO MBEDI AFFAIR

A police summons is never read in quite the same way as a love letter. When it arrives, one can never completely suppress a slight start of fear, even if it's only some routine affair.

Such reflections were perhaps far from springing up beneath Madame Tina's thick wig on a certain morning when, blooming forth in the full freshness of a dazzling new outfit, she walked away from her pretty little house in the Nkondongo section of town.

In addition to her identification papers, she had armed herself with 15,000 francs. A few days before, the driver of her taxi had received a ticket for blocking a public thoroughfare. "Certainly," she said to herself, "it's a question of paying a fine by default! Pshaw, a routine affair!"

But the point in question was to know if there has ever been such a thing as a purely routine affair as far as the police are concerned; a simple request for information had been known to catapult an unfortunate citizen toward unknown destinations. . . .

The taxi dropped her off. With a brisk and lively gait, Madame Tina climbed the five steps to the main entrance; then she plunged into the bowels of that mysterious building, the Central Police Station. She headed directly for the window where uncontested fines were paid. After reading the summons, an officer of the law got up and requested Madama Tina to follow him.

Suddenly, a vague fear took possession of her. Behind the firm mute strides of the policeman, she seemed to glide along, her high-heeled shoes tapping out a nervous tatoo. They ascended one staircase and then another. They went down the long, third-floor hallway; then the policeman stopped in front of a door and knocked. . . . Madame Tina read a nameplate, and she understood. . . . Her heart began to beat furiously. She remembered that she had stubbed her foot on the asphalt pavement as she was crossing the street a few moments earlier.

She didn't like banging her left foot against the ground that way. Every time it happened, she anxiously expected to receive a piece of bad news. No, she didn't like it at all! But she told herself that her day had dawned under favorable auspices. First, a firefly had taken pleasure in flitting about her room all night long. Then, her grandmother, who hadn't a tooth in her head when she died, appeared completely rejuvenated in her dreams. Good signs. . . !

The officer of the law held the door wide open, and his eyes invited her to enter; a miserable little shiver kept gnawing at her spine.

A bureaucrat about forty years old, clean shaven and shrouded in an ash-gray suit, sat enthroned behind a large, luxurious, and meticulously polished desk. After designating a chair for the lady, he read the summons and asked in a neutral tone of voice, "Are you really Madame Tina?"

Madame Tina scowled before sitting down. Then she prepared a timidly engaging smile and grumbled almost as an aside. "Astonishing . . . ! The honorable Police Chief Engamba no longer recognizes me! Truly astonishing! One would be tempted to say that. . . ."

She swallowed the end of her sentence and mechanically shook her head.

Police Chief Engamba had just lit a cigarette. With his eyes plunged into a dossier which he read page by page, he began to smoke in short puffs. He raised his head and allowed an interrogatory glance to sweep over her. He gave the impression that he was ransacking his memory, asking himself where in the world he had seen her before. An amused smile wandered over his lips, while he seemed to be thinking, "Incredible, these great ladies in the city of Yaounde! They sometimes imagine that the chic of their dress will cause such a stir that everyone will be duty-bound to recognize them. When will they learn that respectable citizens have more to do than that? Such women barely succeed in giving pleasure to the eye as long as permanent applications of outrageously expensive beauty aids permit them to glisten like flowers before they wilt and die. And because they know themselves admired by those who run after legs and shapely figures, they believe they have the right to be as popular as the nation's heroes. . . ."

"Look, madame," he finally said out loud, "the exercise of my duties constantly places me in contact with so many people that I can't possibly recognize them all. Unless. . . . unless personal relationships bind me to a certain number of them."

"That's exactly the case for me!" the lady squealed triumphantly, and placed two large smiling eyes on display.

"What. . . !"

"You're not going to tell me, Mr. Engamba, that you've never set foot in my house, that you've never had a drink in my house, that you've never slept at my house . . . ! With my cousin Catherine! Your little Catho. . . !"

In the mouth of a black African speaking good French, this familiar but counterfeit mode of address has a tendentious ring.

"Well, well . . . !" exclaimed the chief of Police. "It's been such a long time that . . . . How is my little Catho?"

A self-satisfied smirk passed across Madame Tina's face. She riveted a pair of mischievously smiling eyes on her counterpart. She wanted to reply. Especially in the hope of gaining a little sympathy and creating an atmosphere suffused with intimacy. Especially too in the hope of dissipating that vague feeling of anxiety which had overcome her in his enormous room with its sombre wall hangings . . . . . Alas, she didn't have time.

Whether, by means of a profound shrewdness acquired during his experience-filled career, he had accurately divined the elegant lady's intentions, or whether, obedient to his professional conscience, he was in a hurry to fulfill his civic duty while avoiding any needless waste of time, Police Chief Engamba continued without waiting for her response:

"OK. . . ! Madame Tina, I have been placed in charge of a little investigation. You have been invited here to reply to my questions. The affair doesn't concern you directly. You just need to supply a few facts. They will help the police in unravelling a mystery. You are a respectable citizen of good repute. I'm therefore counting on your honesty and candor. With your permission, let us begin with a verification of your identity."

As the lady listened to his words, her eyes were popping out of her head. She handed him her identity card. She bit her lip and rested her crossed arms on the edge of the table.

"Ever been convicted?" inquired the police chief, after having jotted down her particulars.

"Me? Convicted. . . ? Well, if the fines I so frequently pour into the coffers of the State are convictions, then, yes, I've already been convicted many times!"

Her reply was made in a defiant, almost indignant tone of voice. One might almost have said that she felt wounded in her self-esteem. People don't like to be asked if they have been convicted. A word to the wise for all policemen . . . !

"What did you do in 1955?" resumed the police chief, whose features remained as expressionless as those of a public executioner.

Madame Tina's face wrinkled with the effort of remembering. "They should have carried out their little investigation of me before sending that miserable summons!" She passed a discreet glance over the calendar attached to the wall; it indicated the date as January 21, 1966. She asked herself what she could possibly have done eleven years ago that was serious enough to evoke so much interest at the police department.

107

In 1955. . . ? She was only twenty at the time. her mother was already dead, and her father had been afflicted with blindness. Like any young girl who had reached that age and possessed no visible means of support in Yaounde, she had somehow managed to keep body and soul together . . . . What could she have done that evoked so much interest at the police department? Suddenly, a half-forgotten memory occurred to her: "Oh!" she exclaimed with feigned indifference, "A routine affair, Your Honor. A senseless quarrel and a few blows exchanged at some dance-hall. A little matter of jealousy. They took both of us to the police station in Messa, and both of us were sentenced to pay a 1,000 franc fine! Reconciled, we were allowed to leave . . . . But what does that harmless, ten-year-old business have to do with anything now, Your Honor? Did the other woman. . . ."

"Far from that," he interrupted drily. "Simple formalities. Tell me the truth, Madame Tina. The whole truth, and nothing but the truth. Simply answer each of my questions. It's part of an investigation requested by the Prime Minister himself! If you tell me the truth, we will soon be finished."

108

Madame Tina was shaken with palpitations of the heart, and they momentarily took her breath away. The whole importance of the affair became clear to her for the first time. Could His Honor, the Prime Minister, order the investigation of a routine affair? And then, what sort of intercourse had she ever had with that person of consequence who, what's more, she only knew by name. . . ? Mouth agape with astonishment, she sighed and then whispered in a taut voice. "His Hon-or, the Prime Min-is-ter!"

The temperature was quite normal in that enormous room. But Madame Tina felt goose-flesh creeping over her body. She had the impression that a thousand fans had just been turned on. His Honor, the Prime Minister! Her head was filled to bursting with these words, the content of which seemed to set her brain on fire.

*

*   *

In our large cities there is a feverishly expanding class of women who like to consider themselves highly respectable members of society. These ladies occupy a special place in the antheap world of single, liberated, and quite public women; they would hold it against you for the rest of your life, if you ever used the degrading word sapak* in reference to them. As far as they are concerned, the true sapaks are all crammed together in the odious promiscuity of the slums, where anybody can pick them up in any old way and where they earn, in the end, the disdain of everybody.

But they themselves . . . ! Deeply concerned with their social standing, these women proudly appropriate the fine-sounding appellation "Madame" for themselves while remaining utterly contemptuous of the more wholesome duties attaching to this noble title.

To perfume themselves with the scent of respectability, they move in among the honest citizens. Once there, they select their customers from the higher spheres of society, bleed the most fat-bellied pocketbooks, and calmly accumulate their unearned savings. No, you'd better not place these grand unmarried ladies on the same roster as the sapaks, for they inscribe their own names on each sunrise as a way of making the whole world realize the stage of evolution that the African woman had reached. . . !

After the fashion of women in her walk of life, Madame Tina had never sunk to the level of restricting herself to a single life's companion. She told herself that marriage is nothing but another form of slavery. Thus, she feared seeing her freedom of action taken from her, and she feared seeing the field of her activities diminished. After having tried three marriages and lost two divorces, she permitted herself to adopt a mode of existence in which women are accountable to no one. Thanks to her beauty and her sharp intelligence, she had become wealthy. A house built mostly with solid bricks, a taxi, European furniture, chests full of pleated skirts. . . .

By arousing envy, she had attracted a goodly number of married women to the lusory rewards of marital infidelity. . . . She owed nothing to anyone! And above all,

---

S.A.P.A.C. is the acronym of a fish company which originally sold its produce at very cheap prices. By extension, it became a slang term for a lower-class prostitute.

there had never been the slightest commerce between herself and that celebrated His Honor, the Prime Minister. . . !

His Honor, the Prime Minister . . . ! "Perhaps a rejected lover, some important government functionary, is playing a dirty trick on me?" She was still pondering to herself, as Police Chief Engamba continued to riddle her with impertinent little questions. In particular, he wanted to know if she knew a certain Sango Mbedi. What did he mean to her? Why did he come to her house so frequently. . . ?

Madame Tina started. That name "Sango Mbedi" stunned her. It was as if she had just been beaten with a heavy club. She seemed to fall into a daze. "Sango Mbedi. . . ." That name by itself raised the curtain upon a less than glorious episode in her own life. She coughed and cleared her throat, before beginning to speak in a choked voice.

Two months earlier, she had met Sango Mbedi one day in the street. In complete disarray and nearly unrecognizable, he calls out to her, comes over to her. He informs her that he is a trusty at the Central Prison. She easily guesses the reason. . . . In her eyes, Sango Mbedi no longer represents anything more than a cocoa-nut emptied of its clear white fluid! To cut short a conversation which offers little prospect of accruing to her profit, she invites him to pass by her house sometime. An evasive invitation and extended only out of simple politeness. But she is forgetting that a man in prison is a man in need.

Believing that he had been given the green light, Sango Mbedi begins once more to frequent her assiduously. Not as the happy lover of bygone days, but as a needy soldier of fortune, drawn to this woman of the world by a few grudgingly offered meals and packages of cigarettes. And that was all.

Madame Tina falls silent. Doesn't she have anything else to say . . . ? The police chief obliges her to speak by asking her point-blank, "and that money embezzled from the State? Are you going to say that you don't know anything about that . . . ?"

She stared with her large, *pinari**-outlined eyes. She was beginning to see more and more clearly what this affair was all about. She had been summoned to these austere premises not as a well-known, respectable citizen, but as the presumed accomplice of a civil servant charged with the embezzlement of public funds. She asserted that she knew nothing at all about money embezzled from the State. And in a scarcely convincing tone of voice, she added: "You must understand, Your Honor, it was out of simple charity that I invited my former lover to come to my house from time to time. For me, he was nothing more than a human being in distress. Not the slightest intimacy existed any longer between us! Furthermore, you men claim that we women love only for money. I'd like to prove just the opposite."

The police chief's eye twitched slightly; the trace of a smile crossed his lips. He repeated that it would be in her best interest to tell the truth, the whole truth, and to aid the police in clearing up a mystery. . . .

Heart fluttering, she listened with one ear. Clear up a mystery. . . ! What mystery? she asked herself. She rested her head on her hands as if to reflect more deeply, and then

---

*an indigenous cosmetic powder used as an eye shadow

waving three fingers in the air, she swore on the three persons of the Holy Trinity that Sango Mbedi had concealed nothing at her house. Raising her voice, she suggested, "It would even be in the best interest of everyone concerned, Your Honor, if you proceeded immediately to a thorough search of the house!"

"Ah-hah!" burst out the Police Chief, contorting his lips into a skeptical smile. "Surely, Madame, you had some inkling of this little investigation before you came here today. Thus, you must have swept your house from top to bottom! So that in the case of a search, the police would find nothing there! Not even a suspicious pin! Isn't it true, Madame?"

She felt literally terrorized by these words. Was she going to have a serious affair on her hands for the first time in her life? She thought of all those innocent people who were rotting away in the squalid gloom of prisons for the simple reason that they couldn't establish conclusive proof of their innocence . . . . If the same fate came crashing down on her! She was the only bread-winner in her family. Her blind father, her young child. . . . Tears welled up from the depths of her eyes. But she did her utmost to hold them back. She was ashamed to cry, telling herself that tears were inappropriate to a lady of her social position.

"Very suspicious, Madame Tina. Your invitation to a house-search is very suspicious," resumed the Police Chief coldly. "You know perfectly well that the police would not find anything there! Not even a picture like this one! Isn't it true, Madame?"

Saying that, he produced a photograph. It didn't take long for Madame Tina to recognize her image next to that of Sango Mbedi. Love sometimes leaves its telltale signs.

"Not even a scrap of paper like this one! Isn't it true, Madame?" continued the Police Chief, as he took a sheet of paper from the dossier. "It is in your interest to talk, Madame . . . !"

It was awful. . . ! Madame Tina began to see red. A tremor passed across the surface of her skin, moving in all directions at once. There was a buzzing in her ears. A cold and stinging sweat trickled down her armpits. She could no longer believe her eyes.

If was awful. . . ! Between his thumb and his forefinger, the Police Chief was holding a sheet of paper across which was crawling Madame Tina's own delicate and wizened handwriting. And that sheet of paper—she recognized it. To tell the truth, the Police Chief knew as much if not more than she did about that shady Sango Mbedi affair. She'd certainly have to tell him everything she knew about it.

"Ex. . .excuse me, Your . . .Your Honor," stuttered Madame Tina in a quavering voice. "Excuse me for having thought at first that such things wouldn't interest you. For it's a matter of . . . ."

"There is nothing, Madame, which is not of interest to the police!" growled Police Chief Engamba for the first time as he interrupted her. "It is in your interest—I repeat— to tell the truth, the whole truth. . . ."

*

*   *

The salaries received by all African functionaries make them, beyond any shadow of a doubt, the privileged and spoiled children of their respective countries. Nevertheless, some of them can't refrain from plunging their greedy arms up to their armpits in the coffers of the State. Truly, they have chosen a bad way of amusing themselves . . . ! In Cameroon, the Special Criminal Court is not amused. It comes down hard on offenders. It sends them somewhere to reflect more seriously about what should be understood under the rubric of national independence! And *that* can sometimes last more than ten years.

No, it's nothing to laugh about when a man who has eaten his bread for a long time beneath the sunny skies of freedom is suddenly cut off from his people, torn away from all the pleasures of fashionable society, and precipitated without transition from a soft mattress onto a wooden plank bristling with uneven rough spots. Nothing at all to laugh about. . . !

Thus, it was not without reason that Sango Mbedi, indicted for "embezzlement of public funds," entertained painful misgivings. One day he asked Madame Tina if she knew anyone who could get him out of trouble. His benefactress advised him to engage a lawyer. He observed that, even with the most illustrious attorney, it seemed impossible that his innocence could be established by the simple, classical means of pleading "not guilty." The only solution, he suggested, was to consult a "professor."

Madame Tina thought of Mami Benedikta. That woman knew more than one witch-doctor's ruse. Madame Tina owed it to her that she had become the mother of a child. But in regard to Sango Mbedi's case, she had to acknowledge a lack of competence. For that reason, she conducted Madame Tina to the residence of

Professor Oguruwu in the Briqueterie. Brrr. . . ! the name alone represented a miracle of pronunciation!

Heeding the proverb which asserts that "a mature banana tree is known by its leaves," Professor Oguruwu swept Madame Tina's sartorial splendor with a speculative glance and concluded that he had to do with a person whose purse was "mature."

"Only 200,000 francs with an advance payment of 60,000 francs. . . ! Yes, merely 200,000 francs and that only on account of Madame Benedikta. Otherwise . . . . "

Madame Tina breathed in her lower lip and bit it in astonishment, 200,000 francs! But why *only?* Was that a negligeable sum . . . ? Ah well, after all, she said to herself, what are 200,000 or even millions of francs when it's a matter of recovering a human being's liberty?

Professor Oguruwu explained that the required advance would permit him to buy certain rare perfumes which had the power to attract a legion of gnomes encamped at the base of Mount Koupé . . . These gnomes were supposed to scour the dossiers of all cases presently before the court and to destroy the one pertaining to Sango Mbedi, down to and including the least memoranda of transmittal.

This initiative filled Sango Mbedi with joy. As far as paying the advance was concerned, he promised to have one of his aunts, who supposedly kept watch over his savings, come up from Douala. In vain, Madame Tina waited for Sango Mbedi's aunt. In vain, Professor Oguruwu waited for a 60,000 franc advance . . . ! The annoying thing was that Sango Mbedi no longer set foot in Madame Tina's house. . . .

"And that was a great satisfaction to me, Your Honor. I was afraid of being implicated in that embezzlement business. Two weeks later, I explained the new state of affairs to Madame Benedikta when she appeared early one morning on my doorstep. She was accompanied by Oguruwu, who was fuming with anger. He revealed that he had bought all the necessary perfumes at his own expense and that he had already mobilized his gnomes. They were soon going to be on site in Yaounde, and he didn't know how how to receive them in a manner worthy of their dignity. For they subsist on nothing but white hens and yams from Kalabar. . . ! He threatened me with the wrath of his gnomes. He feared, according to what he said, for my life . . . ! I too was very much afraid. I was trembling with fear, and that's why I engaged myself, Your Honor, to pay him the 60,000 franc advance out of my own pocket! But alas, I had to admit that I didn't have enough money at my disposal . . . !"

"And this list, Madame? You haven't yet said anything about it!" placidly intervened the Police Chief, who seemed to have followed her story with only one ear.

At that point, Madame Tina burst into tears. It had been composed in her handwriting under Professor Oguruwu's directions, and her eyes were now afraid to encounter it again — that incriminating list across which her delicate and wizened handwriting crawled like a battalion of little caterpillars and where the names and titles of the country's highest officials were deployed in imposing and majestic order. . . . From the President of the Republic to the local magistrate, and including the Prime Minister, the Minster of the Interior, the Minister of Justice, the Attorney General and the Chief Justice of the Special Criminal Court. . . . Oguruwu's gnomes were supposed to search the offices of all these dignitaries and to render the Sango Mbedi affair null and void on every level.

However, it was necessary to make an advance payment of 60,000 francs.

Madame Tina did not reply. The Chief of Police looked fixedly into her eyes, while his own sparkled alternately with vexation and pity. Was he trying to tranquillize her somewhat jangled nerves? Perhaps. He lit a second cigarette and, while continuing to smoke, said in a surly tone of voice:

"All the worse for you, Madame, if you persist in hiding something from me. I'm telling you again that you're not implicated in all this. Your duty is to help the government get to the bottom of the affair."

"I have told you everything, Your Honor," she said in a tearful voice, "And I swear to you that I've been open and frank."

"Half-way, Madame! For if I hadn't shown you the incriminating picture and the list. . . ."

Police Chief Engamba interrupted himself. The ensuing silence was oppressive for Madame Tina. What should she do now? She was like a sick woman who, having just vomitted profusely, feels that she is carrying an immense void inside her, that her very bowels have been disgorged. . . . Yes, Madame Tina had thrown up everything. And the Chief of Police was asking her to throw up again, and again. . . . For a moment, the temptation to make up a story seductively caressed her spirit. But she thought better of it; she feared that an invented story might precipitate her onto all-too-slippery ground. How could she make her innocence as plain as day? Mentally, she addressed a prayer to the Holy Spirit. But suddenly the thread of her pious reflections was severed by a start of fright, as a disconcerting question fell like a pole-axe from the lips of the Police Chief. "What is your political persuasion, Madame?"

114

She was dumbfounded, incapable of whispering the slightest word. What? To ask her that, she who had a phobia about everything relating to politics! Hang it all . . . . As a woman of the world, her only concern was that of eating well, dressing fashionably, and making herself up artfully so that she might always appear beautiful and charming. What business did she have getting mixed up in politics? What exactly was he getting at, this Chief of Police? She succeeded in relaxing her lips and, visibly offended, she replied in a furious tone of voice: "Is that the reason why you invited me here, Your Honor?"

"As I told you from the very beginning, Madame, your duty is to answer all my questions. It's not up to you to direct yours at me."

The Chief of Police had also become offended, and he had spoken with those harsh intonations which sometimes characterize the speech of people who hold the officially sanctioned power of government in their own hands. The lady uttered a brief, embarrassed sigh and then mumbled in a resigned but respectful tone of voice: "In any case, Your Honor, you make me ill by asking such a question! There isn't a political opinion in my head! And for a very good reason . . . . In that domain, my religion is a closed book! I know brothers who have been separated forever by politics . . . . I know all sorts of people who have been prematurely killed by politics! Yes, the very worst gift which the white man palmed off on our young countries is what they call politics. Politics is the cause of all our present hatreds and all the many sorrows which continue to burden our young hearts. That's why I hate politics and politicans . . . !"

"Ah-ha, so then you hate the Chief-of-State and his Ministers!" Police Chief Engamba shot out, as an unfriendly smile creased his lips.

"Ah, no! No. . . ! It's their proper duty—the Chief-of-State and his Ministers — it's their duty to be involved in politics. But I'm speaking about the others."

"What others?"

"The others. That is, the ones who aren't in power and who turn over heaven and earth to replace those who are bent on remaining in power! That's where the first spark comes from, Your Honor, and then fire, and then hell itself. . . !"

The Police Chief continued to flash an ill-natured smile. An inexhaustible flood of questions and insidious comments flowed from his mouth.

"Just a moment ago, Madame, you said that there wasn't a political opinion in your head. And here you are in the process of expressing one . . . , which isn't bad at all."

The lady scowled, and a burst of righteous indignation heaved in her bosom; with an audacious and furious edge in her voice, she retorted: "But why ask me the question in the first place? You know very well that at present all Cameroonians have the right to but a single political opinion! Besides, there's no choice to be made. And besides . . . and besides, they should leave me along with their politics. . . ! Me, I don't belong to any political party."

She had become agitated. Almost without knowing it. Having become aware of what was happening, she regained control of herself, fell silent, and nervously began to bite her reddened lips. Inwardly, she regretted having made such a compromising disclosure; it placed her too far down the slippery path of politics.

After having surveyed Madame Tina with an enigmatic glance, the Police Chief muttered harshly, brutally: "Why do you persist in hiding it from us, Madame Tina . . . ? Why, huh? You yourself have just revealed that you don't belong to any political party . . . ! Not even to the great party of national unity . . . ! But here at police headquarters, we know that you are the moving force behind a secret cell of the U.P.C.* and that you and your fellow conspirators are trying to overthrow the government in power. . . ."

Madame Tina raised her arms heavenward in a gesture of protest; propelled by her amazement, she sprang up and then, falling back into her chair, emitted a tremendous shriek from her feeble woman's throat—a shriek which echoed through every corner in the Central Police Station.

"Don't pretend to be surprised, Madame!" bellowed the Police Chief impassively. "If something bad happens to you, you have only yourself to blame! I told you once, and I told you again that the Prime Minister attaches great importance to this matter; I told you that it's your duty to denounce everyone who is plotting against the established institutions of the nation! They are the ones who are using you like a pawn on their own chessboard. They are the ones who sent you to consult the witch-doctor Oguruwu in the Briqueterie; and you are the one who turned over to him a list of all the leaders of State he was supposed to assassinate by occult means! The list, here it is . . . !"

While he was growing angry, Madame Tina trenbled and perspired; her mouth hung open, and she panted nervously. She had heard all those words without understanding them.

"The U.P.C. . . . ! What was the U.P.C. doing here . . . ? A thousand tombs! That political party still hasn't finished swallowing up innocent victims in it's mighty fall, has it? No doubt I'll soon be among them. Who has been able to survive the accusation? No one! Chiefs. *lamidos*,** rich businessman, priests, representatives in the national assembly and even ministers have been seen sweating blood or giving up the ghost for having been accused, justifiably or not, of being involved in a U.P.C. affair! All the more reason that I, poor single woman that I am . . . . To think that I only wanted to live peacefully, far from all political squabbles! then this! People are right when they say that politics in our country is like a maze of stagnant puddles after a rainstorm. Try as you might, you can never avoid them all. And here I am, right in the middle of a political quagmire, when all I was thinking about was living peacefully, far from all political squabbles. Who could have hated me so much as to hang that on me. . .?"

Madame Tina was inwardly bemoaning her lot. She recalled all those worthless scum who, like flies on spoiled meat, infest the bars and night clubs of the ghetto and who at the drop of a hat will flaunt their status as secret agents, threatening you at the top of their lungs, "Do you know who you're dealing with?" Perhaps one of them might have . . . .

---

*Union des Populations du Cameroun, a clandestine movement which originally fought against French colonial rule and later opposed the post-Independence government of President Ahidj

**the rulers of large areas in Moslem North Cameroon

Her willpower abandoned her. She was no longer ashamed of letting tears streak her pretty, painted little face. Oh, how a beautiful woman's features become ugly when covered with tears!

"Poor me, a poor single woman! If I only had a husband . . . ! Because I don't belong to anyone, I don't have anyone to protect me against the storms of life! Which of my casual lovers would be so imprudent as to compromise himself on my account in an affair involving the U.P.C. . . . ? Poor me!"

Seeing the Police Chief turn to one side and press a button which rang a bell outside, she stopped talking and wiped her eyes. Her whole body was shaking. Her heart filled with anguish as it drummed out the preceding chain of events; she waited, telling herself that it was all over for her.

*

*   *

The room's enormous door swung on its hinges. A totally unexpected scene emerged before the tearful lady's very own eyes. It made her dizzy. In front of a policeman, there appeared the silhouette of a person rather eccentrically decked out in a gandourah, which though apparently new was torn in places and covered with splotches of mud. It was Professor Oguruwu, who must have been treated a bit roughly by the police. Madame Tina didn't understand anything about the whole business. She closed her eyes for an instant. Oguruwu made his entry. . . . Handcuffed and gnashing his teeth, he swore by all his grand and glorious gods; he shouted like a devil imprisoned in the bottom of an ice-box, but all that emerged was a gibberish which was neither French nor English.

"Me no unnerstan, Mista Guvna! Na so Governman Camaroni he go give me mercy. . . ? Na me sef be go for see Mista Prim Minista, be say him sum peoples for U.P.C. wan make coup dey tat. . . ! Na so Governman Camaroni he done give mercy for sum man who be look good for 'em? Me, good Nidjerian. Me done come for Cameron do good ting and not bad. . .! Me magic be good magic. Me magic no kilam sum body. Dis Madame, she done give me name for Mista Pres'den and Minista for kilam! Done gimme aussi plenni money! Na so, me say no, Mista Guvna, and me no unnerstan. . . ! Na so Governman Cameroni he done give mercy for sum man who be look good for 'em?"

It was incredible. . . ! The Nigerian's voice boomed through the entire room as if it were a magical trumpet into which all the gnomes of Mount Koupé were blowing. And it never paused.

Madame Tina burst out in desperate sobs and then in scandalized expressions of indignation; then in furious oaths, in pleading gestures, in horrible shrieks. . . . And as if she no longer knew how to pronounce a single treacherous word of French, she cried out from time to time in her native tongue: "Whayi ma ai awu ya, emot nyo. . . ? Menga bo wo dze. That man over there, why do you wish death upon me? What have I done to you?"

She wanted to boom out in a loud, stentorian voice. To drown out the witch-doctor Oguruwu. To make herself heard and to fling a curse-filled denial into his face.

Alas, her strength and will-power were gone . . . . That strange individual exercised a diabolical sway over her, and with a pitiful expression on her face, she could resign herself to do nothing but cry.

She cried, while Oguruwu, staring at her from time to time with a fascinating look in his eye, pitilessly railed against her with every iota of strength in his vocal chords. . . .

"Dis Madame, she done gimme plenni money for kilam Mista Pres'den and Minista: Me say no, Mista Guvna, and me no unnerstan! Na so Governman Camaroni he done give mercy. . . ."

118

Sniveling sorrowfully, Madame Tina whispered, "Does God exist? If God exists, is He truly just? And if He is just, is He truly all-powerful . . .? No, if God existed, he couldn't be just and all-powerful at the same time, for if He were, He wouldn't permit con-men and a whole breed of criminals to pursue their activities with impunity! He would strike them down immediately to prevent them from harming innocent people . . .!" Despairingly, Madame Tina implored God to intervene on her side against the witch-doctor Oguruwu, but, often taking God as his own witness, the witch-doctor Oguruwu roared vigorously against Madame Tina, heaping damning accusations upon her.

While the fellow continued to bay like a drunkard in his own backyard, Police Chief Engamba pierced him with a glance alternatingly quizzical, sceptical, and hostile. Then all of a sudden: "Shut up, Oguruwu, . . ." he scolded harshly. "You have acted only out of spite. You simply wanted to avenge yourself upon this woman, for if she had come to pay you the sum of 60,000 francs, you would never have gone to see His Honor, the Prime Minister to denounce a political conspiracy. And that conspiracy, as you know better than anyone else, exists nowhere except in your own money-grubbing imagination. And the letter addressed to Madame Benedikta proves it. There you insist upon asking her to brook no delay in exercising her influence upon Madame Tina so that the sum in question might find its way to you, a condition which, if not fulfilled, would prevent you from working for the immediate release of Sango Mbedi. . . that letter, here it is!"

The Police Chief triumphally brandished a sheet of paper. Then, with a legitimate fury resounding in his voice, he continued scolding all the more harshly.

"Professor Oguruwu, you thought the Police of Cameroon were nothing more than a band of imbeciles! Don't believe it . . . ! A closely supervised investigation of this affair has been carried out. Thus, you never had much of a chance to succeed in all your financial machinations. And because Cameroon has no need of foreigners like you, you'll be deported within twenty-four hours. . . ."

Madame Tina had been listening to all this with a slightly apprehensive feeling of satisfaction. The Police Chief lowered his voice and, turning toward her, said with a tone of authority: "As for you, Madame, you will be subject to house-arrest for one month. I hope you will use the time to reflect more seriously upon the credence that should be accorded witchdoctors and their subversive packs of lies. . . !"

THE TRUE MARTYR IS ME
(a previously unpublished story)

THE TRUE MARTYR IS ME

The last shades of night had barely lifted in the village of Nsam. A fifty-year-old woman left her hut. Supporting herself on a cane, she walked over to a little neighboring house, planted herself in front of the door, and began to shout: "Edanga. . . ! Edanga. . . ! Get up. Edanga . . . ! You have more than five river-crossings to make . . . ! Get up so that you can be on your way . . . !"

Not the slightest sign of life from the interior. The woman approached, and rapping her little cane on the barricaded door, she began again: "Isn't there anyone in this house then? It seems silent as a grave. Could Edanga have left already without taking anything with him?"

She broke off, having heard the creaking of a rattan bed.

"Aha. . . ! Are you there then, Edanga, still asleep? How many legs do you have, eh? More than five river-crossings and with that basket on your head . . . ! Get up, Edanga. Now is the time to be on your way. When traveling by foot, people quickly get tired in the heat of the sun!"

Inside, a voice grumbled disgustedly. Then, with a great creaking of the lock, the door opened, permitting an approximately thirty-year-old man to emerge. His pants had been patched repeatedly, and his shirt was covered with mud splotches. Without looking at the woman, he sank down upon a log; his features were drawn.

"What's wrong, Edanga?" she became worried.

"Where's the basket, mother?" he muttered, and that was his only reply.

The woman regarded her son for a moment before wending her way back to the hut. When she returned, she was dragging an enormous basket pleated with palm leaves. She deposited it in front of him. Once more she disappeared into the hut and returned with a good-sized rooster and a hamper filled with assorted parcels.

"Go get yesterday's stalk of bananas. I can't carry it. It's too heavy. Don't forget to take the yams as well. These days your wife must be begging, if she wants to stay alive at Mbankolo. It's been many moons since you've been there."

Edanga complied, dragging his heels. He came back and placed the stalk of bananas and the yams in the bottom of the basket. Then he sat down again on the log;

he was holding his head between his hands, and his gaze was lost in space. His mother could not understand why he was in such a bad mood. He had always been happy and gay, especially when it was a question of going to Mbankolo. With slow, labored motions she began to arrange the food, all the while sighing; "Here's the package of ground nuts, and here's the cucumber . . . ! Here's the packet of sesame seeds, and here's the one with the spices. . . ! There are also several bunches of onions and a little calabash of palm oil. . . ! In this package, there's some smoked fish; it could crumble into little pieces, if you aren't careful how you carry the basket. . . !"

If there had been a witness to this scene, he might well have asked who the woman was talking to. Frozen into a posture of complete detachment, her son only had eyes for the surrounding vegetation, still bathed in the misty shadows of dawn, and he only had ears for the dissonant chorus of frogs, toads, crickets and birds greeting the sunrise with their carefree songs.

"Good, that's it, Edanga! You can leave now. You can tell your wife that I'll do my best to come see her some day myself."

Edanga's mother had said it with a hint of triumph in her voice, as she finished tying up the basket with banana-tree fibers and carefully placing the good-sized rooster on top.

A moment later, like a slave who intends to obey only his own whims, the young man stood up ponderously. He stretched and ill-humoredly inspected the enormous, food-swollen basket with his eyes, before bending down . . . .

"What're you doing, Edanga?" said his mother suddenly, as an idea crossed her mind. "Today is Sunday, and you want to leave for Mbankolo like that? Without washing up? Without changing clothes?"

"You're getting senile, mother!" scolded the young man angrily. "I know old people of your age who don't talk such nonsense! To get me out of bed so early, when the basket hadn't even been loaded yet?"

Before the dumbfounded eyes of his mother, he tested the weight of the basket, lifted it, and placed it on his head. He was just preparing to get underway, when an almost completely bald old fellow shot out of a nearby hut and began to take his turn at scolding: "Who are you so impudently accusing of senility, Edanga? My wife may be old, but yours who is so young and beautiful—where is she? If you were a man worthy of that name, she wouldn't still be imprisoned in the *sixa** after three years . . . ! And all that simply because you can't pass the catechism examinations . . . !"

"Aie-Kai-yai, father!" cried Edanga with respect and fear. "I didn't insult my mother. . . ! All right, don't tease me about that. I'm going . . . !"

"Yes, go, and be quick about it!" bellowed Edanga's father as he brandished his fly-swatter, "My daughter must be dying of hunger at Mbankolo . . . ! Look at his get-up! It's that of a convicted criminal! Do people pay visits on their loved ones in such filthy costumes. . . ?"

Swelling in turn with threats and mockery, the paternal voice railed on as the young man disappeared around a turn. He walked along a pebble-strewn road, his head

*a compound in French African missions, where engaged women received spiritual instruction before marriage. See "Introduction," pp. xix-xx

burdened with thoughts of martyrdom beneath the heavy basket of food, on top of which the good-sized rooster intermittently trumpeted a royal cockadoodledoo, as if to accentuate Edanga's torments.

It wasn't the first time that Edanga had gone to the Catholic Mission at Mbankolo. He had gone there many times during the last three years. A twenty-kilometer walk with a heavy load of food on his head eventually became an onerous burden to him. The last time was six months ago. On that day, he'd found the women of the *sixa* in a coffee plantation. Covered with sweat and under the supervision of an elderly catechist, they were clearing the land with blunt machetes, dulled by long years of toil. As they worked, their tearful voices intoned this popular lament:

> Skin and bones,
> I've become skin and bones,
> Skin and bones like a ripe fruit withering on the vine,
> Never having been relished by a loving tongue.
>
> I toil in the fields of Lord *Fada**
> I toil for whole moons and whole seasons,
> And my spine grows old with it,
> Yet Lord *Fada* doesn't love me,
> And when I'm told that the race of *Fadas*
> Never long to see a woman's skirt,
> I know that I'm toiling in vain,
> Toiling for nothing,
> Toiling to harvest nothing.
> When shall I toil then,
> Oh, my mother,
> In the fields of one who loves me?

Edanga had slipped behind a bush and made a sign. Having caught a glimpse of him, Angoni had asked permission to go shake his hand and receive her provisions. Immediately, a switch whistled through the air and flattened itself cruelly on Angoni's tender skin. Then a scolding voice: "What conduct! Who deceived you into thinking that you're out here with me to find ways of committing a sin against the sixth commandment, eh? Get back to work, and be quick about it!"

Tears in her eyes, Angoni went back to work. Edanga could not prevent himself from crying at the sight of his fiancee's tears. "Did I pay the bride-price for my beautiful Angoni to watch her being mistreated by just anybody?" he asked himself, trembling with rage. Alas, what could he do but chew the cud of his bitterness in silence? No one had ever dared raise a hand against a catechist, even in the country's most unenlightened village. And all the more if he were the catechist in charge of the *sixa*. No

---

*a pidgen corruption of the English "Father."

one! That would have meant provoking the wrath of the *Fadas*. And God alone knows whether a *Fada* might not be more respected and feared than a white Commandant. People feared the white Commandant because he had brutal guards armed with long sticks that spit lightning. But a *Fada*, think about it . . . ! Not only was he of the same race as the white Commandant; he was also God's representative on earth. Not any old God, but the one who had made white men superior to black men!

Already boiling with a desire for vengeance, Edanga felt his blood turn to ice at these thoughts. Thus, completely crestfallen and defenseless, he withdrew from the coffee plantation to go, like everyone else, and wait for his fiancee in the visiting-room at the Mission.

The visiting-room at the Mission was a plank enclosure that witnessed countless uneasy whisperings, hastily blurted words, and half-formed tears. At four o'clock every day, it became animated with pairs of fiancees. There, separated by a cruel wall which it was forbidden to cross, engaged couples chatted, hardly able to see each other through the peepholes in the wall. And what chats they had . . . ! The old catechist marching ceaselessly back and forth, his ears pricked up like those of a sheep dog. If in all this chirping he overhead a few words he considered obscene, he would cry scandal, separate the offenders, and sometimes even threaten to delay the formal celebration of their marriage. For that reason, each couple continued to speak softly, like saints—that is, without prattling about love or exchanging amorous smiles. The women adopted a more reserved attitude. In their faces one could not see the passion which renders the world's ugliest fiancee beautiful in the presence of her beloved. Their eyes were fixed in glassy stares, like those of elderly widows who no longer expect anything from life. What sorts of pleasantries can two fiancees exchange in front of interlopers? All of a sudden, an enormous bell was tolling loud enough to split your eardrums, calling all the occupants of the *sixa* to evening prayers. And as each quest withdrew from the cursed visiting-room, his heart was consumed with a throbbing grief.

On his return journey, after this mockery of a conversation, Edanga must have astonished anyone who saw him pass. Every once in a while, he'd stop abruptly in the middle of the road, brandishing an angry fist in empty space, shaking his head, clapping his hands, or simply raising three fingers into the air and shouting, "that's the last time!"

He had sworn never again to set foot at Mbankolo with a heavy basket of food on his head only to return alone, tormented by grief and far from his beautiful Angoni. Three years his heart had been bleeding in an endless wait for her whom he had chosen as his life's companion. Three years . . . ! Night and day, the image of Angoni haunted him, invaded him in the form of a melancholy obsession. He had a wife, but he was vegetating in celibacy. He might have understood, if Angoni had rejected his marriage proposal. He might have understood, if, for one reason or another, Angoni had been held back by her parents. But that his beloved should remain imprisoned for more than three years in the *sixa*! He wracked his brain to understand it and to find some justification for it. He recited his catechism like a parrot, but it was all in vain, for never after any of the numerous examinations did his name appear on the list of successful candidates! Yet the dowry had been paid in full. Moreover, after the negotiations which accompany any engagement, Angoni had in fact been handed over to him. However, she was not destined to live with him at Nsam for more than three months.

Yes, three months; that is to say, until that day when the priest of Mbankolo, who was on tour, arrived with a great deal of fanfare. In front of the entire assembled population of Nsam, the missionary became red-faced with anger as he began to rail against the old man, Edanga's father: "What a scandal to let your child live in a state of mortal sin with his fiancee! You have but a short time left to live on this earth, and yet you are doing everything you can to earn a passage to hell! Do you know that all those sins your son is committing against the sixth commandment redound upon your soul? Do you know that?"

"Yes, *Fada*, I know it!" Edanga's elderly father muttered, trembling with fright.

He had trembled with fright to see a vision of himself in the other world, being fed into that immense furnace where all those who failed to toe the line in this world would burn forever and ever, according to the decrees of the Holy Roman Church. . . .

That day had been a day of mourning for the two fiancees. His eyes swollen with masculine tears and his body dripping with sweat, Edanga had thought he would go mad with grief! He felt an invisible dagger bite into his heart. But when he was somewhat cured of his mental sufferings, he had resolved to learn the catechism by heart in order to regain his beautiful Angoni, who had been carried off to the *sixa* by the priest of Mbankolo. . . .

Turning over in his head the troubled past, Edanga asked himself as he was walking, "What is it exactly that they teach those women in the *sixa?* What more than a few scraps of catechism, while making them work like beasts of burden! Besides, the worst of it is that a certain number of them wake up one fine morning to find their stomachs bulging with the fruits of adulteries that go unpunished. . . !" His legs no longer belonged to him. They moved forward, stumbling more and more frequently. Each time they knocked against a stone, he cried out, "And there you have it! Even the stones in the highway have sometimes had enough of being stepped on by those who pass by!" And he told himself that he too had had enough of groaning beneath the cruel regulations of those people at Mbankolo.

Without having noticed either the weight of the heavy basket or the distance travelled, the young man suddenly recognized the Catholic Mission perched on the summit of a hill, there with its Church, its plantations, its *sixa* and its mysteries. . . . He plunged down a narrow path. When he arrived at the market-place, he set down his burden in an unoccupied corner and hastened to unwrap it. Then, having arranged all the produce in front of him, he lost no time in selling it all at half price. With the profits from this discount sale in his pocket, he fled into a nearby bar, where he ordered a liter of red wine. Soon, it seemed to him as if his blood was circulating with a vigor and a courage unknown to him since the day of his birth. It was in this singular state of well-being that he ascended the hill and walked toward the church, which was already buzzing with pious voices.

He sat down on a pile of adobe bricks in the main courtyard. From time to time he got up and craned his neck, keeping his eyes fixed upon the visiting-room. Once in a while, in front of the horrified and shocked eyes of the faithful, whose late arrival had obliged them to follow the mass from outside, he made a great show of urinating next to the Holy House of God. Then again, he could be heard grumbling and waxing indignant over a Mass that kept dragging on. Finally, to his great satisfaction, the church doors opened, discharging a flood of people into the surrounding area. Suddenly, he got up. Running at full speed, he dashed toward the visiting-room, climbed the plank wall like a madman and suddenly found himself in the forbidden enclosure. His heart was beating as if to break open his chest. He waited . . . . Several minutes later, the nuns passed in front of him; they remained silent but were obviously astonished to see a person of the male sex in a cloister reserved for women. Then an endless line of fiancees flowed in. Edanga's eyes appeared to be popping out of his head as they rested first on one face and then on another . . . . All of a sudden, cries of amazement echoed in the sky, and a stampede broke out among the women. Edanga had sprung forward to grab one of them by the arm. And before they could regain their composure he had dragged her toward the visiting-room and smashed the plank wall to pieces with a single powerful kick, and now there he was outside the enclosure with his beautiful and charming Angoni.

"From this day, on," he barked, "You will no longer sleep here, far away from me! You will no longer sleep here in this slave camp invented by colonialist missionaries! You are my wife, and you must stay with me at Nsam!"

Edanga never stopped barking, while Angoni, who was caught fast by the arm, advanced in self-defense. She trembled, shouted, cried, called for help . . . . It wasn't that she no longer loved her fiancee. But the abduction seemed so strange to her, so scandalous, that she couldn't prevent herself from trembling, shouting, crying, and calling for help.

While all this was taking place, the elderly catechist who was in charge of the *sixa* came running. He seized the young woman by the other arm. Then during a quarter hour of universal merriment, there ensued a tug-of-war in which the beautiful Angoni fell, first to one side and then to the other, while her heart-rending screams pierced the air.

For an instant, Edanga stopped pulling and shouted at the catechist, "What do you think you're getting mixed up in, eh?"

He released his hold on Angoni and fell upon the old man, thrashing him soundly and throwing him on the ground to the accompaniment of repeated peals of laughter. All the young men regarded Edanga with admiration. To them, he was a liberator of future husbands and, above all, a liberator of all the women in the *sixa*. "What cruelty to deprive men of their wives for years! What injustice . . . !" they yelled on every side. Only the other catechists took it into their heads to champion the cause of their senior, who looked as if he had just been dragged from a flour sack. But they entered the fray at their own peril. Beneath the weight of irresistible blows of the fist, each of them suffered an identical fate.

Suddenly, the peals of laughter ceased. All eyes were riveted on a white silhouette emerging from somewhere down there and clearing its way through the crowd. It advanced with long loping strides, as the sleeves of its cassock were being rolled up. It was the priest of Mbankolo. This missionary was about forty years old, and he had the reputation of being a regular Goliath. This was largely because he never hesitated to use the white man's pugilistic arts to silence the most boisterous mouths in his parish. That's what earned him the nickname *Fada-Boxer*. He grabbed Edanga by the collar of his shirt; then, after having shaken him violently as if he were nothing more than a garden snake, the priest dealt him such powerful blow that, once released, Edanga tottered for an instant and fell flat on his face. Edanga had just found his master. He lay there in a disconcerting immobility; everyone believed he had fainted. But all of a sudden, he was on his feet, towering to the full height of his man's body. He raised his two hands to his face, pressed his tear-filled eyes, and then ripped off his shirt.

130

"I want my wife!" he began to shout at the top of his lungs. "Nothing more than my wife Angoni, for whom I have paid the bride-price in front of witnesses. . . ."

Seated on the ground, Angoni sobbed mutely but incessantly. Edanga saw her and ran in her direction. But just as he was taking hold of her arm again, the boxer-priest overpowered him and covered him with a shower of blows. Edanga released his hold on Angoni. Drawing himself up, he saw a large red face. He shouted an oath of war. He advanced toward the missionary. He circled his adversary, while patting one of his pockets from time to time. Then, he suddenly plunged his right hand into it. When he raised his fist, a metallic glitter rose with it and inscribed a semi-circular arc in space before disappearing into the folds of the cassock. It was in vain that the boxer-priest tried to subdue the young man's arm, which moved mysteriously, frenetically in a back-and-forth motion. They watched the boxer-priest weave about on his sturdy legs and, with one hand resting on his stomach, collapse onto the ground as a long drawn-out moan issued from his lips. A thunderous chorus of exclamations resounded, almost loud enough to make the church walls come tumbling down. The panic-stricken spectators had stopped laughing. Like sheep unexpectedly overtaken by a windstorm, they ran in every direction, continually jostling against each other.

"He killed him! He killed him!"

"Tell somebody to notify the white commandant. . . ! Arrest him! Arrest him . . . !" they were yelling in every corner of the courtyard.

But no one dared arrest Edanga. He was no longer a man, but a wild animal foaming at the mouth and spitting blood—a wild animal leaping about and running in all directions at once as he brandished a blood-stained dagger in the blinding, mid-day sun.

"Today will be the last day for anyone who comes near me!" he shouted from the depths of his rage-congested lungs. "Where is Angoni, my beautiful Angoni, for whom I have paid the bride-price in front of witnesses?"

Angoni had disappeared. Like all the women of the *sixa*, she had fled, trembling in horror, to find a secure hiding place.

Half an hour later, an automobile arrived like a whirlwind, trailing a halo of dust in its wake. As it screeched to a halt beside the motionless body that lay on the ground, it made a war-like sound. The white Commandant and his guards emerged. Before they could even ask who had committed the crime, accusing fingers where already pointing at Edanga, who alone remained at the scene; increasingly distant voices competed with each other to proclaim: "There he is! There he is!"

A swarm of hands seized hold of Edanga. Then, handcuffed and beneath a hail of punches, whip lashes, and blows from wooden clubs . . . .

"I only wanted my wife, my wife Angoni, for whom I paid the bride-price in front of witnesses—my wife who has been held prisoner for the past three years . . . ! And everyone saw how the *Fada* hit me first . . . ! Look at my bloody mouth! All that because I wanted my wife Angoni, my wife for whom I paid the bride-price in front of witnesses.

The young man was shouting at the top of his lungs and crying; he could be heard calling out to several young people in the crowd, inviting them to testify against the boxer-priest! But no one dared come forward. They all moved away and prudently ducked behind their neighbors, admonishing him: "Keep us out of your affair!"

"Don't do anything to him, commandant!" exhorted the priest, playing out his mournful role, "I. . . am . . . dying . . . a martyr . . . !"

132

Several minutes later, the autombile drove away. It was carrying Edanga who, though trussed up like a giant human sausage, continued to howl incessantly, "The true martyr is me! The true martyr is me.. . . !"

WORKS BY PHILOMBE

Philombe, René (pseud. for Louis-Phillippe Ombedé). *Africapolis*. Yaoundé: Sémences Africaines, 1976. (drama)

_____. *L'ancien maquisard*. Unpublished ms. (novel)

_____. *L'amour en pagaille*. Yaoundé: Sémences Africaines, 1974. (drama)

_____. *Le blancs partis, les nègres dansent*. Yaoundé: Sémences Africaines, 1974. (poetry)

_____. "Le Cameroun en quête de sa pernnalité culturelle." *Cameroun Littéraire*, n. 4 (April 1971): 1-2. (essay)

_____. *Les époux célibataires*. Yaoundé: APEC, 1971. (drama)

_____. "L'écrivain camerounais face à ses responsabilites civiques." Unpublished ms., 1977. (essay)

_____. *Hallalis et Chansons Nègres*. 1964; rpt. Yaoundé: Sémences Africaines, 1973. (poetry)

_____. "Halte à notre étouffement culturel." *Cameroun Littéraire*, no. 6 (June 1971): 1-3. (essay)

_____. *Histoires queue-de-chat*. Yaoundé: CLE, 1971. (short stories)

_____. *Lettres de ma cambuse*. Yaoundé: CLE, 1965. (short stories and anecdotes)

_____. *Le Livre camerounais et ses auteurs*. Yaoundé: Sémences Africaines, 1984. (literary history)

_____. *Nkrumah n'est pas mort*. Yaoundé: private, n.d. (poetry)

_____. *La passerelle divine (Légende Camerounaise)*. Yaoundé: APEC, 1959. (adaptation of folktale)

_____. *Petites Gouttes de Chant pour créer l'homme*. Yaoundé: private, n.d. (poetry)

_____. *Peuple debout, monstre sans age*. Yaoundé: private, n.d. (poetry)

_____. "Le pont des retrouvailles." *Cameroun Littéraire*, n. 9 (Sept. 1971): 1-3. (essay)

_____. "Quinze jours d'un voyage-éclair en Allemagne de l'Ouest." *Dialogs*, n. 1 (June 1980): 11-13. (Bulletin de l'Institut Goethe.) (essay)

_____. "Réponse à Charles Ngandé." L'avenire de la poésie camerounaise. *Abbia* 5 (1964): 167-171. (essay)

_____. *La saison des fleurs*. Yaoundé: private, n.d.

_____. *Sola ma chérie*. Yaoundé: CLE, 1966. (novel)

_____. *Un sorcier blanc à* Zangali. Yaoundé: CLE, 1969. (novel)

WORKS ON PHILOMBE

Bessala Ngo, Louis-Germain. *La Vie et l'Oeuvre de René Philombe*. Unpublished DES thesis: Université de Yaoundé, 1973.

Bjornson, Richard. "Interview avec deux écrivains camerounais." *Abbia*, nos. 31-33 (1978): 213-224.

Brière, Eloise. "La littérature camerounaise: nouvelles tendances ou faux espoirs." *Peuples Noirs – Peuples Africains,* n. 9 (1979): 69-80.

Fouda, Basile-Juléat. "René Philombe: Mage humanitaire des temps nouveaux." *Ozila,* n. 11 (March 1971): 3-5.

Kerker, Armin. " 'The Bald Songstress' Means Nothing to Me" (interview with Philombe). *Afrika* 21, n. 2-3 (1980): 38-40.

Tales From Cameroon contains fifteen allegories, anecdotes, and short stories by the talented Cameroonian writer René Philombe. Composed over a twenty-year period, these charming and witty narratives offer a socially critical yet profoundly human glimpse of what constitutes day-to-day reality for millions of people in the cities and small towns of West Africa.

Philombe's plays, novels, and essays have long been admired and loved by his fellow countrymen, but, because his works were all locally published, they have not until recently attracted a larger international audience. This relative lack of recognition outside Cameroon is unfortunate, for Philombe possesses a unique capacity for seizing upon characteristic details and dramatizing them in a way that embues them with a larger symbolic significance.

Behind each of his works is the temperament of a man passionately committed to unmasking the hypocrisies, foibles, and injustices that plague much of contemporary Africa. Yet, Philombe's voice is neither bitter, nor dogmatically self-righteous; it is one that seeks to reconcile his deeply felt attachment to Africa with a yearning toward universal brotherhood. Philombe is a master of French prose style, and his subtly ironic turns of phrase are nowhere more effective than in the finely crafted pieces of this volume.

As a journalist, book-store owner, farmer, and man of letters, Philombe has exerted an enormous cultural influence in his native country, but his most important contribution has been an unwavering defense of humane values in the face of oppression—first by French colonial authorities and later by the independent government of Cameroon. On numerous occasions he has been imprisoned for speaking out against the abuses of unjust regimes, and during the mid-1950's he contracted a debilitating disease that left him paralyzed from the waist down. His courageous battle against oppression and personal suffering has earned him an almost legendary status among the younger people of his country. One might almost say that he has become their symbol of integrity and decency in a corrupt society.

In the late 1970's, while Richard Bjornson was teaching at the University of Cameroon, he met Philombe and became so intrigued with his short stories that he began to translate them for his own amusement. Convinced that they would be of interest to the English-speaking world, he continued to work on them when he returned to the Ohio State University, where he is currently Professor of French and Comparative Literature. Bjornson has published many books and articles on European and African fiction; he has been a Fellow at the National Humanities Center, President of the American Literary Translators Association, and a visiting professor at universities in France, Germany, and Africa. His translation of the famous Cameroonian writer, Mongo Beti's *La Ruine presque cocasse d'un polichinelle* is being published by Three Continents as *Lament for an African Pol* (1985).

ISBN 0-89410-314-8; -315-6 (pbk)   LC No: 84-50629

Three Continents Press
1346 Connecticut Avenue N.W., Washington, D.C. 20036